GHOST CANYON

Borgo Press Books by JOHN RUSSELL FEARN

1,000-Year Voyage * *Account Settled* * *Anjani the Mighty: A Lost Race Novel* (Anjani #2) * *Black Maria, M.A.: A Classic Crime Novel* (Black Maria #1) * *Bury the Hatchet* * *A Case for Brutus Lloyd* * *The Crimson Rambler: A Crime Novel* * *Death in Silhouette* (Black Maria #5) * *Don't Touch Me: A Crime Novel* * *Dynasty of the Small: Classic Science Fiction Stories* * *The Empty Coffins: A Mystery of Horror* * *Fool's Paradise* * *The Fourth Door: A Mystery Novel* * *From Afar: A Science Fiction Mystery* * *Fugitive of Time: A Classic Science Fiction Novel* * *The G-Bomb: A Science Fiction Novel* * *The Genial Dinosaur* (Herbert the Dinosaur #2) * *Ghost Canyon* * *The Gold of Akada: A Jungle Adventure Novel* (Anjani #1) * *Here and Now: A Science Fiction Novel* * *Into the Unknown: A Science Fiction Tale* * *Last Conflict: Classic Science Fiction Stories* * *Legacy from Sirius: A Classic Science Fiction Novel* * *The Man from Hell: Classic Science Fiction Stories* * *The Man Who Was Not: A Crime Novel* * *Manton's World: A Classic Science Fiction Novel* * *Moon Magic: A Novel of Romance* (as Elizabeth Rutland) * *The Murdered Schoolgirl: A Classic Crime Novel* (Black Maria #2) * *One Remained Seated: A Classic Crime Novel* (Black Maria #3) * *One Way Out: A Crime Novel* (with Philip Harbottle) * *Pattern of Murder: A Classic Crime Novel* * *Reflected Glory: A Dr. Castle Classic Crime Novel* * *Robbery Without Violence: Two Science Fiction Crime Stories* * *Rule of the Brains: Classic Science Fiction Stories* * *Shattering Glass: A Crime Novel* * *The Silvered Cage: A Scientific Murder Mystery* * *Slaves of Ijax: A Science Fiction Novel* * *Something from Mercury: Classic Science Fiction Stories* * *The Space Warp: A Science Fiction Novel* * *A Thing of the Past* (Herbert the Dinosaur #1) * *Thy Arm Alone: A Classic Crime Novel* (Black Maria #4) * *The Time Trap: A Science Fiction Novel* * *Valley of Pretenders* * *Vision Sinister: A Scientific Detective Thriller* * *Voice of the Conqueror: A Classic Science Fiction Novel* * *What Happened to Hammond? A Scientific Mystery* * *Within That Room!: A Classic Crime Novel* * *World Without Chance*

THE GOLDEN AMAZON SAGA

1. *World Beneath Ice* * 2. *Lord of Atlantis* * 3. *Triangle of Power* * 4. *The Amethyst City* * 5. *Daughter of the Amazon* * 6. *Quorne Returns* * 7. *The Central Intelligence* * 8. *The Cosmic Crusaders* * 9. *Parasite Planet* * 10. *World Out of Step* * 11. *The Shadow People* * 12. *Kingpin Planet* * 13. *World in Reverse* * 14. *Dwellers in Darkness* * 15. *World in Duplicate* * 16. *Lords of Creation* * 17. *Duel with Colossus* * 18. *Standstill Planet* * 19. *Ghost World* * 20. *Earth Divided* * 21. *Chameleon Planet* (with Philip Harbottle)

GHOST CANYON

A CLASSIC WESTERN

JOHN RUSSELL FEARN

WITH MATTHEW JAPP

THE BORGO PRESS

MMXIII

GHOST CANYON

FIRST BORGO PRESS EDITION

Published by Wildside Press LLC

www.wildsidebooks.com

DEDICATION

To the memory of Nini Japp

CONTENTS

CHAPTER ONE

It was nearly sunset when Terry Carlton loped his weary sorrel over the rise. Then he drew rein and sat motionless. For a while horse and rider were part of the flaming vermilion sky, vignetted by the towering rocks at the fringe of Pinga Mountains.

Terry Carlton was as tired as his mount. The journey he had covered had been a long one, through the midst of burning sun with few water holes. And now he had gained a rimrock overlooking a small, unmapped town. For a long time Terry Carlton sat gazing at it thoughtfully.

"Guess I never heard of this burg, Smoky," he murmured, and his mount pricked up his ears. "Nothing queer in that, though: dozens of these sorta places scattered around."

He cuffed up his dusty Stetson and considered the scenery. In the immediate foreground on his left were the mountains, their bases already purpling with the coming of night. To the right were the endless stretches of the desert. In the distance lay pastureland—rich, verdant, greying in the evening—and beyond it a town of sorts.

It looked ramshackle, like all these Western outposts, and indeed something more. It had an oddly deserted aspect. There should have been some sign of lights; in the buildings of the main street, Kerosene flares ought surely to have been glowing here and there.... But there was nothing.

"Mebbe a ghost town," Terry murmured, flicking the reins. "Not that it makes any odds: just as long as we can settle for the night.... On your way, Smoky."

The animal began moving again, down the long, dusty slope which led into the valley. The gloom intensified as the last dying rays of the sun were cut off by the mountain range. By the time Terry had reached the trail which led to the town's main street, only a few minutes separated him from the sudden intense dark of the Arizona night. HR slowed the horse's pace, staring ahead, still baffled. It looked as though the town was completely empty. Not a soul, not a movement.

"Keep goin'," he murmured, and the horse obeyed. Then, as he came to the halfway line on the main street, Terry realised he had been mistaken. There *were* lights, but they were nearly obscured by heavy wooden shutters closed across the insides of the windows. This in itself was one of the most surprising things Terry had yet struck. In the dozens of Western towns he had seen, none had ever had shutters.

There were lights behind the windows of the big Black Coyote Saloon—which had top-to-bottom swing entrance doors instead of the normal half-size batwings.

There were lights, too, behind the shuttered windows of several of the dwellings. The general stores, however, together with the livery stables and the various offices of law and order—if any—were completely unlighted.

"Queer," Terry said, half aloud. "Darned queer." He was debating the idea of pulling up outside the Black Coyote and going in for a drink when a sudden distant fan of light caught his eye. It came from the doorway of one of the small shack-like dwellings at the far end of the street and only lasted for a matter of seconds; then it expired again and the darkness was complete.

"More chance of a bite to eat there, fella, than drinkin' on an empty stomach," Terry muttered. "Might as well see what gives."

He nudged his mount onwards, then dropped wearily from the saddle when he reached the gateway of the solitary wooden dwelling. In the darkness which had now dropped, he could see few details beyond the whiteness of the building's front. Tying Smoky to the gatepost, he went up the short path, then up the steps to the screen door. He knocked sharply and then dropped a hand to his single .45, just in case.

There was a long pause. He knocked again. He couldn't be dead sure of it, but he thought for a moment that he saw the white outline of a face looking at him from a lower window, as though the shutter had been drawn back and the light extinguished behind. Then came sounds of movement, the glow of a lamp through the glass of the door behind the screen—and finally a dark-headed girl, the lamp held at shoulder level, came and looked out onto the porch.

"Yes?" she asked quietly, and Terry gave a little start as he saw she was holding a gun steadily. She looked as though she might know how to use it, too.

"Er—beggin' your pardon, ma'm." Terry raised his hands and touched the brim of his dusty hat as he did so. "I'm askin' for a night's rest for myself and my horse, an' mebbe some grub and coffee. I can pay for it and I'll bunk anywheres: in a stable if need be."

The girl said nothing. Her gun remained pointed. Terry looked at her intently. The lamp revealed well-cut features and a very straight nose. Her mouth and chin were decisive; her eyes seemed black or dark blue. She, for her part, saw only a six-footer with lean, powerful hands, and narrow hips, a friendly grin on his young but craggy face.

"You don't speak like a saddle tramp," she said, "yet that is what I assume you are?"

"You don't speak like most of the dames—I mean gals—one meets out here," Terry countered, a twinkle in his grey eyes.

"I had an education of sorts—in Columbus." The gun lowered and, in a different tone, the girl added, "Come in."

"Thank you, ma'm."

Pulling off his Stetson to reveal curly, ginger-tinted hair, Terry stepped past the girl into the narrow neck of hall, then, as she closed and bolted the doors, he followed her into a cosy, oil-lit living room. There was a fair supply of furniture, a skin rug or two, the inevitable shutters over the window....

A big fellow, sixtyish, got up from a rocker and stood by the fire, eyeing Terry intently.

"Howdy," Terry said, smiling and extending his hand; then he frowned as the upright older man took no notice. "It's all right, Dad," the girl said, laying the revolver on a side table. "He talks pleasantly. Obviously not one of the usual type around here. Er—this is my father," she added, as Terry waited. "The name's Marchland. I'm Hilda Marchland."

"Terry Carlton," Terry said, as the girl's father now shook hands. "Glad to know you, sir—and you, Miss Marchland."

"What do you want here?" Marchland asked briefly, and a pair of deep blue eyes pinned Terry intently.

"Nothin' more than a meal and a chance to bunk for the night. Then I'll be on my way."

"Where are you headed?"

Terry shrugged. "No place in particular. I used to be foreman at the Tilted K in Montana, but I got sore with the boss and took to the trail. Since then I've just wandered around usin' up what I'd collected of my payroll. I've come clean across Wyoming, Utah, and Nevada. Now I'm in Arizona. When my money's gone, I'll settle. I kinda like to wander."

Marchland compressed his lips. He looked a fierce old devil, with the high cheekbones and reddish skin of a North American Indian. Possibly it was in his ancestry somewhere. Then when he grinned to reveal big, rugged white teeth, there was a complete transformation.

"Okay, son—stay till you're rested. Guess I've no objections. My gal'll see to a meal—an' your horse. You left it outside?"

"At the gatepost, sir."

Marchland nodded and looked at his daughter. There was a certain relief in her expression. She stepped forward into the lamplight and Terry settled a problem which had bothered him. Her eyes were not black but deep violet, like her father's.

"Fix things up, Hil," her father said. "I'll have a word with Mr. Carlton while you do it. An' don't forget your gun when you stable his horse."

"Gun?" Terry repeated, startled. "What's the idea? What do you aim to do with my cayuse?"

"Stable it, son, and feed it—like we'd do with any horse." The big fellow was silent for a moment, then added: "The gun's for my gal to protect herself with. Never know around here."

"Oh—I see." And Terry stood waiting and wondering.

There was an atmosphere of complex mystery about everything which he couldn't understand.

"Sit ye down," Marchland invited, and returned to his own rocker by the fire at the same time. "I guess Hil won't be long gettin' some grub together for you."

"Naturally, I want to pay for everything," Terry said, and put his hat on the small rail under his chair.

"Forget it. I know the law of the range as good as anybody: give what you have to the traveller, and if you haven't got anything, wish him luck. Only Christian, I reckon."

"Yeah—and thanks. I wasn't too sure of my welcome when your—er—when Miss Marchland pointed a gun at me round the door. Never had that sort of a greeting before."

"I'll apologise for it right now," Marchland smiled. "It's just that we have to be careful. Might have been—anybody," he finished vaguely.

Terry gave a mystified nod. He realised the big fellow was still studying him searchingly, as though trying to assess just how much good he was.

"So you're moving on?" Marchland said finally, and began to clean out the pipe he'd taken from his shirt pocket. "You're mighty sensible, son. Guess that's what all of us'll be doing before long. I'd have gone long ago, only—well, I guess my roots are mighty deep. Born and bred here in this self-same house. Mother and father died here—an' my wife, when Hil was born. Looks like the good God took one and gave one to sort of even things up a bit. I ain't resenting it; just say it's a bit hard, that's all."

"I'm—sorry," Terry said quietly.

"What for? Life's life, ain't it? I'm not kickin'. Only thing I *am* sorry for is to have to get out of here. But I must—an' Hil. An' everybody, before we're through."

There were sounds of movements in the rear of Terry, and the flutter of a cloth as the girl spread it on the table. Terry frowned and thought for a moment. Then he said: "Can't think why you want to move on, sir. As I rode into town I couldn't help but notice what grand pastures you have around here. Best I've seen for over a hundred miles. Why on earth do you want to leave?"

"Don't want to," Marchland growled. "*Got* to!"

"Bought out, do you mean?"

"No," Hilda said, in the background, setting out crockery. "Because of ghosts."

Terry hesitated for a split second, then he grinned. "Ghosts? Who are you tryin' to kid?"

"Honest truth, son," Marchland said. "This whole territory is hag-ridden, and Verdure ain't safe either. Verdure's the name of this town, case you don't know. Called that on account of the pastureland. Ain't nothing like it anywheres."

"But ghosts—" Terry protested.

"I don't believe in them," the girl said, as though to defend herself, and her violet eyes met Terry's steadily as he turned to look at her. "It's Dad here who thinks they amount to something. I say there aren't such things—and if they're there, it must have a human explanation. Naturally, I don't get listened to. The folks in this town have lived their own little narrow lives for so long they're up to their necks in superstition. Even Dad—sorry though I am to say it."

"I sometimes think I made a mistake in giving the gal a decent education," Marchland mused. "It's made her that she ain't got time for anything outside material things. I reckon ghosts are just as natural as th' wind an' the rain. Specially round here, 'cos there's cause for them."

"Here's your meal, Mr. Carlton," the girl said deliberately, and it sounded as though she were trying to change the subject. But her father was not shaken that easily from his course.

"'Specially round here," he repeated, as Terry set to work on the stew which the girl ladled out for him. "Long ago this was Indian territory. The whites moved into it. There was a massacre of the whites by the Indians. Four whites—all men—vowed that they'd return from the dead and haunt the territory. They died more horribly than all the others in the party. For many years the folk around here have reported seeing four horsemen riding the night—like they came out of the Apocalypse; and just recently they've been seen more'n ever! I've even seen 'em myself."

"Probably four saddle tramps in a hurry," Hilda said in contempt. "You and the Apocalypse, Dad! It's fantastic!"

"There's a parallel for everything I say," her father snapped. "Four horsemen in the Apocalypse. Why not four horsemen here? In each case they're ghosts, ain't they?"

"You ever seen them, Miss Marchland?" Terry asked, breaking a piece of bread.

"Once. Moving fast, away to the south, in the moonlight. But nothing will ever convince me they were ghosts." Hilda moved towards the fire and stood with her back to it. The flames outlined her slender figure in the cheap cotton dress.

"And what's all this got to do with your moving?"

Terry asked.

"Because everybody in town's scared!" Hilda flared back. "Or most of them, anyway. According to the legend of the massacre, the four who swore to come back said they would one day lay this entire territory to waste in revenge for their deaths. It hasn't happened up to now, but everybody's so convinced that it will before long—because the horsemen are seen so frequently these days—that they are moving on. Those that have not yet gone shutter themselves in by night, don't go out except by the byways and alleyways, and always with their guns ready. That's why I met *you* with a gun. It wasn't my idea—it was Dad's."

"You've got to protect yourself, gal!" Marchland insisted.

"With a gun? Against ghosts? What use do you suppose a gun would be?"

There was silence. Something in the girl's healthy contempt for spirits made Terry grin. She noticed it and frowned. "Did I say something amusing, Mr. Carlton?"

"Nope. I was just thinking. You seem to be one alone in a community of frightened people. Or at any rate you *were* one alone. So happens I don't believe in ghosts, either."

The silence came back. Marchland gave an ominous stare, and Terry drank some coffee unconcernedly. "Not to believe in 'em is blasphemous!" Marchland snapped.

"Sorry, sir, I don't agree." Terry shook his head.

"When you're used to riding under a clear sky in the fresh wind you just can't believe in spooks."

The girl came forward at that, her eyes bright. She flashed a triumphant glance at her father.

"Somebody on my side at last, Dad!" she exclaimed; then to Terry she added quickly: "I've been trying for long enough to get Dad to bury his silly superstitions and instead make an effort to find out the *reason* for these phantom riders. Only he won't. In fact, *nobody* will—not even the sheriff, and he's supposed to be the guardian of law and order around here. Everybody's plain scared, and rather than face up to the reality they're all walking out."

Terry became thoughtful as he continued with his meal. "How often do these ghosts appear?" he asked presently.

"Almost nightly at present," Hilda answered. "Sometimes they are at a distance by the mountains; sometimes quite near, but so far they haven't carried out their supposed threat of laying the territory to waste. I don't think they ever will. I think they may be outlaws or range riders who happen to pass in this direction each night. There being four of them superstition attaches to the legend."

"How do you see them if it's dark?" Terry gave a puzzled look. "Are they illuminated or something?"

"They're in white—and their horses are white."

"Yeah—'cos they ain't of this world!" Marchland snapped. "How much longer are you goin' to blaspheme, gal, against things which come from the Other

World?"

Hilda gave him a scornful look; then Terry spoke.

"I guess there are two sides to this business, Mr. Marchland," he said. "All due respect to you, sure, but your daughter's entitled to her opinion and so am I. I don't believe in ghosts, but I won't settle definitely for that until I've had a look for myself. What chance is there of seeing them tonight?"

"Every chance," the girl answered, glancing at the clock. "They usually appear around midnight in the mountain foothills or on the trail which leads that way. I saw them once, and from then on Dad forbade me to leave home at night, After that the sheriff issued an order that everybody was to stay put and shutter their windows and bar their doors during the hours of darkness."

Terry got on his feet and took his gun from his holster. He jerked it open and eyed the loaded chambers.

"This is good enough insurance for me against ghosts," he said. "I'll take a ride around until midnight and see if I can spot anything. I'll soon decide then whether we're dealing with spooks or not."

"I'll come with you," Hilda said, turning to the door which was evidently that of her bedroom.

"You'll stay right here, gal!" her father snapped. "1 gave you an order, an' I mean to see you obey it! If Mr. Carlton wants to go, that's his business, but no daughter of mine is—"

"I'm going, Dad," the girl interrupted deliberately.

"1 mean no disrespect to you, but this is the chance I've been waiting for—to have a man by my side who thinks as I do. As a lone woman trying to knock sense into a lot of superstitious fools, I've had no chance—but it's come now, and I'm taking it. I'll be with you in a moment, Mr. Carlton."

Terry nodded and began to roll himself a cigarette. He looked under his eyes at old man Marchland as he stood frowning into the fire. Finally, he flung himself back in his rocking chair and scowled.

"I don't see you can blame your daughter, sir," Terry remarked, striking a lucifer on his thumbnail. "If these ghost *are* phoney, it lets out everybody in town. They don't need to move on. You said yourself *you* don't want to, so surely—"

"I'm saying no more," Marchland snapped, with a fiery glare. "I just say it isn't right to dabble in things beyond us."

"Yeah?" Terry gave a dry smile as he inhaled smoke. "Never yet found anything that was beyond me. Usually a six-shooter solves more mysteries than any durned sheriff—"

He turned quickly as Hilda reappeared. She had change quickly into a riding skirt and blouse, a leather mackinaw placed slackly across her. Terry's eyes travelled to the gun swinging at her hip as she tied a floral kerchief about her dark hair.

"You wear a gun like you're usta it, Miss Marchland," Terry commented, and she turned to smile at him.

"You just can't afford not to be used to it in this

region, Mr. Carlton." She turned to her father and kissed his forehead. "'Bye for now, Dad. And don't worry so."

He said nothing. Terry gave the girl a glance, then opened the door for her. Together they passed through the hall and presently gained the moonlit porch. A cold but gentle wind stirred about them.

"I'll get the horses," the girl said. "I'd bedded yours down for the night. Do you suppose he'll be able to make the trip, or has he done enough for one day?"

"I imagine he has," Terry said with regret. "Unless you can loan me another one, I'm afraid he'll have to try—"

"I'll fix it," Hilda said, dodging away into the gloom. "I've a mare you can borrow."

Terry nodded and lounged down the pathway to the gate. He opened it and then stood looking down the dark stretch of the main street. It went straight into the black vista of the town. It was a sombre, unnerving scene, the buildings turned into leprous white by the reflected light of the rising moon. It might have been three in the morning instead of around half-past nine.

Then the girl returned, mounted, leading the mare beside her. Terry vaulted easily into the saddle and followed the girl as she turned away from the town and headed instead for the open trail, down which Terry himself had come only a little while before.

In a matter of minutes all traces of Verdure had been left behind, and they were cantering along easily in the fresh night wind, the stars about ready to drop out of the cloudless dome overhead.

Terry glanced about him, determining his surroundings as he remembered them from his ride at sunset. As usual, the Western night was impressive, giving Terry the conviction that he and the girl were alone in the universe. The night wind brought with it the intangible aroma of untamed spaces, the smell of the mesa and desert, mixed also with the scent of pine. There was not a sound across the motionless expanses of brittle-bush to either side of the trail. No sign of activity until a night bird fled close beside the girl's head. Far away, disturbing the silence at last, was the remote bass roar of a mountain lion.

To left and right the illimitable brittle-bush fields rolling into the wastes of the desert: behind, a town full of frightened people. Ahead, the mighty pinnacles of the mountain range, their saw teeth cutting fantastic diagonals and segments into the gleaming backdrop of the stars.

Terry drew a deep breath and smiled to himself. This was life as it ought to be, made even more so by the presence of the girl at his side. He found himself thinking how naturally he seemed to have become acquainted with her; how completely she evidently trusted him to thus ride with him through the night.

They were nearing the mountain foothills when she broke her long silence.

"I've seen the ghost riders more than once, Mr. Carlton," she said, "only I didn't dare say so before Dad. You can see how he feels about such things. Not that I blame him really, since he has never seen anything of the world beyond Verdure— However, to get back to my topic. Each time I've seen the riders they have gone through Star Canyon, over yonder."

She drew rein and pointed. Terry drew up beside her. In the pale light of the rising moon, he studied the foothills ahead. At one point the mountains came down to a lower level and were split in a gigantic 'V', to the very base of which the stars glittered. The actual trail leading into the canyon was as yet indistinguishable from the all-surrounding greyness.

"I've always seen them from a distance," Hilda added. "I didn't dare go too close in case anything happened. Now I have you with me I'll take the risk."

"Thanks for the compliment," Terry murmured.

"I don't hand them out for the sake of it." The girl's voice had its usual directness. "I can tell from your manner and voice that you're not any ordinary saddle-tramp. I feel safe with you. I never have with any other man around here.

"Thanks again," Terry grinned, and he could see her face turned to him in the moonlight. "Let's get nearer that canyon and see if anything happens. You lead the way: I'm foreign around these parts."

Hilda nodded and spurred her mount forward again. Terry kept close beside her, and presently they hit the rocky incline which led to the canyon trail. Before they had moved halfway along its length, however, the girl moved, her horse to one side. Terry followed her through an outcropping of small cedar trees and they emerged again on a higher level of ground studded with rock spurs.

"Here's a good place," Hilda said, dismounting. "We can tie the horses here and then, by lying on our faces at the rimrock over there, we can see the riders if they pass through the canyon."

Terry nodded and dropped to the ground. In another three minutes he and the girl were lying on their faces at the extremity of the small tableland, their heads projecting very slightly over the edge of the rimrock so they had a view of the canyon entrance a hundred feet below. They took care that they were not too far over in case the moonlight silhouetted them.

"Supposin' these riders are *not* ghosts—as I don't believe they are," Terry murmured. "What do you suppose the idea is?"

"To frighten the people of Verdure and the outlying ranches, of course," Hilda answered promptly.

"Yes, but—why? What's the point of doing that?"

"No idea. It's something I never got around to thinking about. I suppose I should have done...."

"If we're to tie things up properly, you should," Terry said; then he became silent again, his gun in his hand in case it might suddenly be needed. He noticed Hilda, too, had her .38 resting in a niche of the rock beside her. She was quite the most replete Western girl he had encountered—unafraid, direct, and yet still a woman.

It was half an hour later, and they were both beginning to feel cramped and chilled through inaction, when Hilda suddenly raised a hand warningly, her whole attitude one of intent listening. Terry listened, too—then, after a while, he heard the far-off drumming of hoofs on the hard-baked earth. Straining his eyes, he peered beyond the chasm entrance to where the rich pasture lands spread right up to it.

"There!" Hilda said abruptly, gripping his arm. "See them?"

He nodded, peered at four white specks visible in the moonlight against the blackness of the pastures. They came nearer, and the hoofs drummed into echoes until the canyon walls began to reflect them.

Terry said nothing, but he was conscious of a little thrill, as he watched the quartet. They moved with a steady precision, dead in line with each other. Had he been at all superstitious, he could have believed they *were* phantoms. Not being woolly-minded, however, he put the quartet's perfect riding down to fine horsemanship and an accurate knowledge of the terrain to be covered, which made for almost military movement.

They came nearer. Riders and horses were visible how as all white. Hats, clothes, horses—white as snow, reflecting the moonlight. They reached the canyon entrance and still kept going. Their eyes fixed on them, Terry and the girl watched. They passed below, moving swiftly, the horses snorting at intervals, then as they went on the sharp twist in the canyon hid them from sight and the echoing hoofbeats died away.

Terry took a deep breath and drew his shirt sleeve over his face. He realised the girl was looking at him intently.

"Well?" she asked, her voice quiet.

"I can sure understand now why the folks think they're phantoms," he said. "First time out it's a bit unnerving. Mebbe the moonlight and the silence. They sure look the part."

"I felt the same way the first time. But you surely don't think for one moment that they're—"

"Ghosts? Hell, no!" Terry got on his feet and helped Hilda to hers. They holstered their guns.

"Good disguise," Hilda admitted, thinking.

"Yeah—but I never heard of a ghost-horse snorting! And I never heard of a ghost-horse making noise enough to echo. If those were real phantoms, they'd go through everythin' and not make a sound."

Hilda gave a smile of relief. "You're the kind of man I've been hoping for, Mr. Carlton! You think things out logically instead of rushing behind shutters and talking rot about the Other World."

"Might as well see where they're headed," Terry added, moving towards the horses. "This business has got to be solved—and quickly—before anything else happens. I can't believe these phoney riders are prancing about in the moonlight each night just for the fun of keepin' a legend going…. Let's move."

His strong arms lifted the girl into her saddle, then he swung up on his mare. Together they returned down the rocky slope they had formerly ascended, and in a matter of minutes reached the canyon floor. Here Terry again dismounted, and the girl sat and watched him as he inspected the dusty hard-baked ground in the moonlight. Unsatisfied, he thumbed a lucifer into a brief glimmer, cupping it in his hands and peering at the ground. As the light extinguished he gave a chuckle.

"What?" the girl asked, as he came over to her.

"Just the fact that those horses have very material shoes," he replied. "Real ghosts wouldn't leave footmarks behind, I guess. Anyways, let's see where we can go by following this canyon."

"I can tell you that right now. It leads straight out to the mesa. After that, there's nothing until the next town of Luna Mucho."

"We'll go, anyway," Terry decided, and swung back into the saddle. This time he went first, his gun ready, Hilda coming up behind him. As he went, Terry watched the surroundings carefully. Once beyond the bend in the canyon down which the horsemen had vanished, the canyon walls came inwards suddenly, until towards the centre of it there was room for perhaps only six horses abreast. From here the canyon widened out again and in ten minutes Terry found himself gazing at the moonlit expanse of the mesa, the canyon trail running down towards it like a zigzagged white ribbon.

"No sign of 'em now, anyway," he said quietly. "I sort of thought there might be, out on the desert there. White against black. It would show."

"Might," Hilda muttered. "Unless they're out of sight."

They became silent. The mystery of the night had closed down again. It was queer the effect it had in these lonely spaces. Even with the physical evidence of horses' hoofs, in the dust Terry somehow felt uncertain....

Struck by a sudden thought, he ignited another lucifer and held it cupped in his palm as he dropped from the saddle. Hilda alighted beside him. He didn't know quite what to think when he found there was no trail of hoofs except those of his own and the girl's mount.

"But—it's silly!" Hilda protested.

"Yeah. Course it is." The lucifer dropped and expired in the dust. "They must have gone straight on because we know they didn't turn back, just as we know they couldn't have turned aside and gone upwards—not with these sheer walls."

Terry looked about him. Three hundred foot high escarpments at this point. No vegetation, no rockery niches, no acclivities. Either the four horsemen *must* have gone upwards, or—?

"I don't get it," Terry confessed finally. "Better go back a bit and see if there's any sign of their trail leading off to some place."

Hilda nodded, and leading their horses, beside them, they returned along the canyon floor. The moon had risen high now. It was possible to see the dust at their feet and the prints their own mounts had made on the previous journey. And presently they came again to the spot where the prints of a whole party of horses had been tramping.

"But look—!" the girl almost whispered, pointing in

the moonlight; and Terry flared another lucifer just to make sure.

He couldn't explain what he saw. It was next to uncanny. The trail of the four horses was mixed with the trail of his own and the girl's horse but, whereas the trail of his and Hilda's mounts went straight on, the others stopped short. Up to a certain point they were clear enough, then, without turning aside, they simply ceased to be.

"Sure is tarnation queer," Terry breathed, as the lucifer died out. "Narrowest part of the canyon, too, where there's no room to move to one side. An' I guess these walls are so steep nothin' could get up 'em. Smooth as a lake, I guess."

The girl looked at him in the moonlight and said nothing. He knew just what she was thinking.

CHAPTER TWO

"I guess we'd better get back into town," Terry said at length. "Nothing more we can do right here, and this wants thinkin' about. Mebbe we can come back in daylight and weigh things up properly."

"Uh-huh," Hilda agreed, and said no more. It was plain she was shaken. She climbed onto her horse and nudged if forward, Terry catching up with her after a moment or two.

Neither of them spoke on the leisurely journey across the pastureland to town. Only when they were back once more in the living room, with Marchland looking at them suspiciously, did they feel they could speak openly.

"Must be some explanation," Terry muttered, frowning. "Four horses an' riders couldn't just vanish into thin air!"

"Huh?" Marchland demanded, getting up from the rocker by the fire. "What's that you say, Mr. Carlton?"

"We saw the horsemen, Dad," Hilda explained. "They leave tracks, just like any horse should—only there's something queer. They vanish into nothing halfway along Star Canyon,"

"What in tarnation else d'yuh expect ghosts to do?" her father demanded. "You ain't got no right to pry into such things, either of you! Lookin' on things of the Other World is blasphemous: I sed it all along!"

"They're not of the Other World, sir," Terry said, musing. "I'll stake all I've got that riders and horses were solid as you and I, but they've sprung a mighty clever trick of disappearing. Makes you think for a minute that they *are* phantoms! I guess the daylight will show how it was done. I'm going back there in the morning."

"And I," Hilda said firmly.

"All right, if that's so there's no knockin' sense into you." The old rancher's voice was grim. "I'll have no part in it, gal. If you die 'cos of your curiosity, that's your own fault. I figger from this, Mr. Carlton, that you're stayin' on awhile?"

"If I may," Terry nodded. "I'll pay, of course."

"Ain't necessary. I told you that earlier."

Terry gave a shrug. Marchland was snappish, that was obvious. He turned to the girl as she stood thinking.

"Long past midnight, gal, in case y'don't know it," he said. "Time we were gettin' some shut-eye. Which room are we fixin' for Mr. Carlton?"

"I'll—I'll fix it up for you, Mr. Carlton," the girl said, starting. "There's a room on the other side of the hall. Come along with me."

"Thanks," Terry agreed, and followed her out.

The room into which she showed him, after lighting the oil lamp, was clean and comfortable and smelled of newly aired linen. He caught her hand and shook it as she turned to go.

"Don't stay awake all night trying to think this thing out, Miss Marchland," he said, smiling. "It'll explain itself."

She nodded. "I hope so. In any case, I'm not so worried over that—puzzling as it is—as I am over father's reluctance to credit there's a material explanation for phantom horsemen. Anyway, see you in the morning. And thanks for being on my side."

Terry patted her arm reassuringly and she departed. He stood for a while thinking; then he blew out the lamp flame and moved over to the bed in the moonlight. A big nightshirt was lying on it for his own use. He grinned as he looked at it: he grinned even more when he'd donned it.

As he got into bed, he made up his mind to lie and think out the problem of Star Canyon—but Nature had other ideas. He fell asleep almost instantly, worn out by his exertions and riding. When he awoke again it was full daylight, the sun pouring its blazing heat upon him through the partly-opened window.

He dressed quickly and then stepped out into the hall, just as Hilda was crossing it with a loaded tray, from which drifted the aroma of grilled ham and coffee.

"Howdy," Terry smiled—and she smiled back at him. Now he saw her in daylight he was surprised to find she was prettier than he had suspected, unless the effect was created by the simple cotton frock she was wearing.

"Sleep well?" she enquired,

"Sure did—ghosts or no ghosts. Where do I shave?"

"You mean *how* do you shave, don't you?" she asked, as he took the heavy tray from her. "Or did you bring a razor?"

"Always carry one, Miss, in my shirt pocket—I'll take this tray in for you. Mighty heavy for a girl like you."

Before she could say anything, he walked into the living room. Marchland was there, sprawled in the sunlight near the window, his rocking-chair going back and forth. Opposite him sat a big fellow, dusty sombrero cuffed on the back of his head. Terry glanced over him and drew his own conclusions from the star badge on the man's shirt.

"This is Mr. Carlton, Sheriff," Hilda introduced, as Terry, set down the tray, "Sheriff Harrison."

The Sheriff rose to his feet, hand extended. He was bigly made, square-shouldered, with twin cross-overs about his waist. Except for the smallness of his eyes, he could have been handsome with his beak of a nose, determined jaw, and brick-red complexion.

"Howdy," he said, as Terry shook hands. "I jus' bin hearin' from Mr. Marchland here that you figger to stay around a bit, stranger?"

"I like the scenery," Terry explained calmly.

"That ain't the reason," Marchland snapped, looking up at him sharply. "You know dog-gone well you're stayin' around so's you can poke your nose into this phantom horsemen business. I say you're loco to even try."

"Guess so," Harrison agreed, with a curiously hard smile. "I wouldn't recommend it, Mr. Carlton."

"I'm naturally inquisitive," Terry responded. "And until I've found out all I want, I'll just stay. All there is to it— Now, excuse me, will you. I must shave."

He turned and left the living room, frowning to himself. He could not decide whether he liked the Sheriff or not. By the time he had finished shaving and was withdrawing his head from the cold water tub he had found in the back garden, he was decided that he did *not* like the Sheriff. He groped around for the towel and found it handed to him. He dried his eyes, and in surprise looked at Hilda.

"I was going to tell you there's hot water in the kitchen for shaving," she said.

"I managed," Terry responded; then, as he noticed her serious expression, he added:

"That *all* you came to tell me?"

"No. It's about Sheriff Harrison." She gave an uneasy glance through the kitchen towards the living room. "I think I ought to explain something. He—er— he fancies his chance with me."

Terry dried his massive forearms. "Congratulations," he said briefly.

"I mean, he may think that you are now standing in his way," Hilda added. "If so, he may become dangerous. He's got a vile temper. I've seen it on occasion. He also has some sort of a hold over Dad. I think that's why Dad is so edgy sometimes. They have innumerable conferences, locked up in the living room. I think one is brewing right now, otherwise Harrison wouldn't have ridden over so early."

"Ridden?" Terry repeated, buttoning his cuffs. "His office is only fifty yards down the street."

"His office, yes—but he's come from his ranch. That's ten miles away out of town—the Falling-J."

Terry hesitated for a moment. "After all, Miss Marchland, it doesn't really concern me what happens to you or your father. I don't want that to sound as though I'm not interested, but I'm only a stranger who has asked for temporary lodgement."

"Can't you understand that I need help?" Hilda asked earnestly.

"How?"

"This ghost business, for one thing: The fact it makes Dad behave so queerly every time the matter is mentioned. Then there is the fact that he keeps thinking of leaving the district, from which I am trying to dissuade him. Lastly there's Sheriff Harrison. I can't bear the man, or his attentions, yet there isn't anybody else I can turn to—or wasn't. Since he's sheriff, most men are afraid of him."

"Thanks for the build-up, Hil," commented the sheriff himself, and Terry and the girl turned sharply to see him lounging in the kitchen doorway looking out into the yard.

"Well, it's all true and you know it!" the girl retorted, her violet eyes glinting as she faced him. "I never asked you to come chasing after me. Anyway, you're too old."

"Seven years ahead of you, Hil, Mebbe," Harrison commented. Then his small eyes moved to where Terry was tightening up his kerchief. "As for you, Mr. Carlton," he added, "I guess you might do worse than hit the trail. Verdure is a mighty dangerous place to be in right now."

"Meaning ghosts?" Terry asked calmly, and he gave an innocent smile.

"Meanin' lots of things. I'm tellin' you plain as I can to get goin'—an' not ter come back."

"Sorry, Sheriff. When I like a place I stick around, and it'll take more than the law to make me move on. It has no legal reason to, so I just stop."

"I figger it isn't that you like the place so much as Miss Marchland," Harrison snapped.

Terry reflected. "Could be. Miss. Marchland's a mighty fine girl—pretty as they come. Too pretty to be pestered if she doesn't want it. Or mebbe you don't know the meaning of the word, no matter how often it's fired at you?"

Hilda looked from one man to the other uneasily. Not that Terry seemed disturbed. With a comb minus several teeth he was smoothing out his unruly ginger hair and smiling impudently. It seemed to rattle Harrison, for he came down the steps and. ambled across, big hands on his gun-holsters.

"Listen, fella," he said deliberately. "I don't know jus' how plain y'want it sed, but you're not welcome around here. Now start movin'—"

On the last two words, his right-hand gun flashed up

into his fingers, but at the same time something else happened. Terry's right hand detoured somehow in smoothing up his hair and crashed in an iron fist under Harrison's jaw. It was one hell of a wallop, and made Hilda wince as she heard it click. The Sheriff hardly knew what hit him. His gun dropped and he was partly lifted off his feet. Stumbling backwards, he caught helplessly at the huge water butt. It overbalanced and deluged him. He lay gasping and spluttering, his jaw feeling as though it were on fire.

Then Terry reached down and, with an easy movement, twisted his fingers in Harrison's shirt front and swung him dizzily on his feet.

"Now listen," Terry said deliberately. "Since I aim to be around this district quite a while, Sheriff—and since I like Miss Marchland every bit as much as you do— we might as well know how we stand. I don't like you, and you don't like me. Okay! Now we know. I'll take no orders from you, and if I choose to roam around, I'll do it. Lastly, you got the idea I wasn't welcome around here. Should be the other way about. *You* keep away from here—or else! Savvy?"

Harrison ripped himself free and looked about him for his gun. He glared when Terry stooped, picked it up, and handed it over.

"A little spoiled by water, Sheriff; otherwise okay," he said pleasantly.

"You think this is goin' t'get you anywheres?" Harrison whispered, his breathing hoarse with fury. "I'll blast you outa town before you're finished, Carlton.

You'll find out what it means to stick around where yore not wanted!"

"Move!" Terry ordered, his grin vanishing and his gun springing into his hand. "Hurry it up!"

Arguing with a loaded gun was evidently not Harrison's idea of fun. He gave a final glare, straightened his sodden hat, then marched angrily back into the kitchen. Terry kept right behind him, and stayed behind him until the sheriff was speeding away down the High Street. With a grin Terry leathered his gun and turned to meet the eyes of Hilda behind him.

"I—I appreciated that," she said. "Dangerous though it may prove later on."

"Dangerous?" Terry gave a grim smile. "I'm not worrying, Miss Marchland.... And how's about some breakfast?"

She nodded and led the way back into the living room. Old man Marchland was already at the table, pouring out coffee. He gave Terry a bitter look as he settled at his. place.

"I guess that wasn't very sensible of you, Mr. Carlton," he snapped. "For one thing, the sheriff is a friend of mine, and for another he stands for law and order around here. It's plain loco to bounce around the man who runs the law."

"I'll bounce *any* man who makes himself a nuisance," Terry replied calmly. "Miss Marchland made it plain that she doesn't like his attentions, so I had to do something—since you won't."

Marchland said nothing. He seemed at a loss. He

gave the girl a glance and then went on with his breakfast in dogged silence.

"Do you still intend to see what happened to those riders last night?" Hilda asked presently, and Terry nodded.

"Sure thing. In the daylight it might be possible to pick up a few clues. The moment I've finished this breakfast I'll be on my way. I'd like you with me, if you can make it."

"Why?" Marchland demanded. "Apart from trying to convince my gal that these ghosts ain't genuine, you have to start running around with her as well. I don't like it, Mr. Carlton."

"She's a free agent," Terry said. "Up to her."

"I'm going," Hilda said. Then she looked at her father sharply. "I wish I could make some sense out of your attitude, Dad. It just sounds as though you *want* to perpetuate this idea of ghost riders."

"It ain't that, gal: I just say we shouldn't dabble. Our best move would be to give a lead to the rest of the people in this town an' be on our way to some other place."

"So you've said for weeks past—ever since the phantoms first came," Hilda pointed out. "But you don't go. Either admit the phantoms are phoney and brave it out—or else get on the move. As it is, you're playing both sides at once."

Marchland got on his feet angrily, threw down his napkin.

"I'll not have my own daughter dictatin' to me what

I'll do!" he snapped. "I'll go when I'm good an' ready: meantime, I'll say what I like."

And before the girl could answer, he left the living room and passed through the hall to the outdoors. Hilda was silent for a moment, biting her lower lip; then, with a shrug, she resumed her breakfast.

"Mebbe I said too much," Terry muttered.

"No, it's not that. It's Dad. He's so touchy, and I can't think why. Or can I? I sometimes believe it's the sheriff who makes him that way. Every time the sheriff's been here's always this sort of trouble with Dad...."

Terry did not take up the matter, because he considered it was not strictly his business. He finished his breakfast, then when the girl had done likewise she said:

"The stables are at the back, Mr. Carlton. If you'll saddle my horse and your own I'll join you in a minute or two. I've got to change. I'd have dressed in readiness earlier on, only I thought that might give Dad too big a shock."

Just what she meant by this Terry was not sure, so he merely nodded, took down his hat from the door, then went out to the stables. He found old man Marchland in the yard smashing sticks with an axe. He stopped his job and watched as, presently, Terry emerged with the saddled mounts.

"Don't have much say around here, do I?" Marchland growled.

"I think you're taking it the hard way, sir," Terry told him. "Surely if all your daughter and I are trying to do is rid this town of its fears, you ought to encourage us, not try and block us at every turn?"

Marchland spat on his hands and resumed chopping without another word. He didn't even look up as Hilda came out in her riding kit. She said goodbye to him, but he took no notice. Her face troubled, she swung to the saddle and followed Terry out of the yard and into the sun-scorched dust beyond the gateway.

They were halfway to the mountain range before Terry spoke.

"Whether these horsemen are phantoms or not, Miss Marchland, our job henceforth is to find out the reason for terrorising the populace. Far as I know, there are usually three things that make it worthwhile getting tough—namely, gold, oil, and water. I have known massacres for those three things. Which of them is it likely to be around here?"

The girl shook her head. "I've no idea. None of them, as far as I know."

"Then why scare the populace?" Terry demanded. "It doesn't make sense without a reason! My belief is that these phantom horsemen are a plant, making use of an old-time legend for a modern purpose. There must be something about the territory around here which makes the game worthwhile."

As the girl merely shrugged, Terry added: "We'll look into it properly when we've seen Star Canyon."

They reached it half an hour later, and began a slow advance, watching the ground as they went. Their own trail and that of the four horsemen was clearly distinguishable now in the blaze of the morning sun—but there was still no gainsaying the fact that at the narrowest neck of the canyon the prints of the quartet just vanished into thin air.

Terry dismounted and considered the sheer granite faces of the canyon sides, spreading out somewhat as they reached the summit. The tops of the escarpments were possibly two hundred feet, bright grey against the cobalt of the sky.

"Nothing could go up there and nothing could turn aside," Hilda mused. "Likewise, we know that nothing turned back. So where *did* those horsemen go?"

"They went *somewhere*," Terry said stubbornly. "Maybe one of these rock faces can swing to one side: I've known that to be possible sometimes."

He knew he was talking for the sake of it, but he began an investigation none the less. It got him precisely nowhere. Though he and Hilda examined the rocks for over an hour, they came to no solution of the mystery. The cliff faces were sheer, unmarred by a single seam, and certainly immovable except by blasting.

"I sure could believe in ghosts if I wanted," Terry confessed at length, mopping his streaming face. "Guess we might go up above and see if anything else shows itself. Be a little less grilling up there, anyways."

Hilda nodded, limp with the searing heat burning down into the canyon. They secured their horses, found the acclivity of the previous night, and mounted to its summit. Fresh wind struck them as they came onto the rimrock and they had a vision of the countryside for miles around. Not that this interested them: their sole anxiety was to find an explanation for four vanished horses and men.

And yet again there was no answer. On the summit here there were rocks by the hundred, of all shapes and sizes, projecting from the mainly flat tableland. But nowhere was there a crack or a seam, or a single clue.

"Might be different over there," Terry said, nodding to the opposite side of the canyon, from which they were separated at this height by a hundred feet of emptiness.

"We'd better look whilst we're at it," Hilda responded, regardless of the blazing sunlight. "We shan't want to make this investigation again."

Terry nodded and they returned to the canyon floor, then went up the opposite side. At the top of this escarpment, the rocks were flatter, but there were no fissures, naturally balanced spurs, clefts, or anything of a nature likely to arouse suspicion. The whole business was as completely baffling as a brilliant conjuring trick,

"It's got me," Terry admitted at last, and sat down with his back to a rock spur to rest. "I just don't get it!"

Hilda settled beside him, fanning herself with her kerchief.

"You don't suppose—" Her voice faltered and a profound look of worry came in her violet eyes.

"That they really *are* phantoms? Not on your life!"

"Then—where did they go?"

"I dunno." Terry looked into sun-drenched distances. "We'll solve it finally. Meantime, we're off on another tack. I'm going into town to the local assayer. I want to see his maps."

"Oh?"

"You see," Terry explained, "the assayer is the one man who has good maps of the district. He has to in his job. I want to find out what there is in this territory that might be worth having if the people could be driven out."

Hilda nodded, then after a while she got on her feet. Terry rose beside her, and together they returned to their horses. On their way down the lonely trail back to Verdure, Terry asked a question.

"Not my business, really, 1 guess, but what does your father do for a living? I don't suppose he keeps that house of yours going on nothing. So—how come?"

"Has that question anything to do with the four horsemen?" the girl, asked directly.

"Could be. I'm just trying to tie up your Dad's queer attitude to our investigatin' this phantom business. I don't like saying it, but mebbe it's to his advantage to keep us *away* from the phantoms."

"Why? You don't suppose he has anything to do with them, do you?"

"I dunno, Miss Marchland. I'm just fishin', I reckon."

Hilda rode on in silence for a while, then she said quietly: "My father's retired from active work. About five year: ago he sold his holdings in the Roaring-J., which he owned. It was a pretty prosperous ranch, but he didn't actually *live* there. As he told you, he's lived in our present home all his life. Acquiring the

Roaring-J through good cattle deals, he put men in to work it, made a good profit from it for several years, and then retired. So he now lives on his savings. How much those savings are worth I don't know. I get the impression sometimes that he's running out of money. Which is one reason, I think, why he doesn't want to pull up sticks and start again elsewhere."

"Mmmm...." Terry reflected as he cantered his horse along. "And you did say you think the sheriff has some kind of a hold over him?"

"It's only a suspicion. Don't think of it as anything anymore."

Terry nodded and said no more, but he did a good deal of thinking as the ride into Verdure was completed. Once in the main street the girl pointed out the assayer's office to him, and they rode towards it. In some surprise Terry contemplated the activity of the place now daylight had come. Men and women were going back and forth along the boardwalks and in and out of the various stores: the shutters had gone from the windows: even the top-to-bottom doors of the Black Coyote had given place to the normal half-pint batwings.

"Will you be safe enough while I'm in the assayer's?" Terry asked, dismounting outside the office.

"I've my gun." Hilda patted it. "Don't worry about me. I'll be okay."

Terry nodded, looped Smoky's reins round the hitch-rail, then went up the steps into the assayer's. The assayer himself was a small, narrow-faced man with steel-rimmed spectacles. He came from behind his private partition as Terry thumped the hinged counter for attention.

"Yeah?" the assayer asked, peering at him. "Somethin' to declare, stranger?"

"Nope—guess it's your turn to declare. I want a look at your territory maps."

The assayer frowned. "I reckon that ain't legal, stranger. Or, leastways, it ain't without Sheriff Harrison's say-so. You'll find his office jus' down th' street—"

"Listen, fella...." Terry's gun was suddenly in his hand. "If I want to look at a map, I'm going to, see? An' don't hand me that bromide about gettin' permission. There's no such law. All you are tryin' to do is be awkward."

The assayer raised his hands slightly and had to back as Terry sat on the counter, swung his legs easily across it, and stood up on the other side. He looked towards the far wall beyond the partition and nodded in satisfaction. As in most assayers' offices, there was a huge, scale-drawn relief map spread out, tacked to the faded plaster wall, a map covered in green and red circles which represented private markings on the part of the assayer himself.

"What the hell's the idea?" the assayer snapped, his mood changing. "What right have yuh to—"

"Shut up and sit down!" Terry gave him a push and he landed with a thump in the worn swivel chair. There he remained, afraid to challenge the .45 which Terry kept in readiness in his hand as he studied the map. Unfortunately it did not tell him much. At length he turned back to the assayer.

"If you've finished, git outa here!" the man snapped.

"I'm not—yet. I want some information which isn't given on this map. What's so valuable in the territory that it's worth drivin' everybody out of it?"

"Huh?" The assayer's eyes widened behind the spectacles.

"You heard, fella." Terry aimed the gun at his forehead. "I guess a lot of folks in Verdure here are plain pop-eyed over a collection of phantom horsemen—even to the extent of some of you quittin'—but I'm an outsider an' ghosts don't scare me none. I figger there's some reason for the set-up and I mean to find it. You're one man whose business it is to know every yard of the territory. So what's valuable around here?"

"There's nothing valuable," the assayer panted. "Yuh can see that from the map! I guess Verdure is one of the few towns in Arizony that ain't worth having. No gold—no oil—not even a water course worth mentioning."

"There's *something*," Terry insisted. "There's gotta be!"

"Cross me heart, stranger. You're crazy. Verdure's one town that ain't worth the land it stands on, apart from grazin'."

Terry relaxed and sighed. He slipped his gun back in its holster.

"Okay," he said quietly. "I don't believe you, but I

guess I'd have to take you apart to make you talk, and you mightn't even then. So I'll find out some other way. Truth of the business is the people of this town are scared to say anything to anybody. Right?"

The assayer gave a shifty glance, and that was all.

"Sheriff Harrison bein' the cause," Terry added, and the look he got satisfied him that he had hit a bull's-eye.

He said no more. Swinging back over the counter, he returned to the outdoors, where he found Hilda still waiting for him on her horse. She aimed a questioning look.

"No dice," Terry said, shaking his head. "Though I do get the impression that that assayer knows a durned sight more'n he's telling. Look, Miss Marchland, just how much power has Sheriff Harrison in this town?"

"Pretty well all of it," she answered. "He, Mayor Burridge, and Grant Swainson seem to run Verdure between them."

"Yeah? Who's Grant Swainson?"

"He runs the 'Black Coyote' down the street." Hilda nodded to the saloon. "Incidentally, he's another man who's always asking me to marry him."

"Is he crooked or straight?" Terry asked.

"I guess nobody's straight in this place if they have power," Hilda answered.

"Three men running a town on gun law." Terry mused for a moment as he swung back into the saddle. "Mebbe I'll have t'do something about that. Seems to me that Harrison, Burridge, and Swainson have got things too much their own way around here. Right now, I reckon we can't do better than return to your home and work out some kind of plan."

Hilda nodded, and flicked her horse's reins. Terry followed behind her, pondering as he rode. In the rear yard of the girl's home he alighted and she preceded him into the living-room. Then, as she crossed the threshold, she stopped dead. A horrified gasp escaped her

"What the—?" Terry began, coming up behind her; then he gave a start and quickly hurried forward.

Sprawling across the skin rug near the fireplace was old man Marchland, face down, motionless. As Terry reached him and turned him over, a tell-tale red stain became visible on Marchland's white shirt.

"Is—is he?" Hilda could not get the words out. Her eyes were staring fixedly.

Terry's hand moved to Marchland's wrist as he felt for the pulse. He looked up grimly.

"'Fraid so," he said quietly. "He's been shot dead—clean through the heart."

The words flung Hilda forward. She gripped her dead father's shoulders tightly, shook him, wept over him. Terry turned away, tight-lipped, looking quickly about the room. After a moment or two he spotted a Colt lying under the table. He lifted it gingerly and broke it open. One bullet had been discharged. Then, as he looked about him, he saw something else—a letter folded once and propped up on the mantelshelf.

He did not cross to it there and then. He waited for Hilda to recover a little from her grief; then he took the folded note down and handed it to her. Her eyes brimming with tears, she read it, Terry looking over her shoulder:

My dear Daughter,

Money troubles and deals of which you haven't known anything make it impossible for me to go on. Had we moved out of town as I'd figured on doing later, we could have straightened out—but since you've decided to take the side of Carlton and stay on that just can't happen. Seeing no way out I've decided to put an end to it.

Always your loving

Dad

The note fluttered from Hilda's fingers to the floor, and she broke into a fresh outburst of weeping. Unable to control it, she dashed to her bedroom, went within, and slammed the door. Terry stood for a moment, then he picked the note up, re-read it, and finally put it away in his shirt pocket. The Colt he wrapped up in a piece of scrap paper from the bureau and stuffed inside his hip pocket. The details attended to, he raised the dead body of Marchland, put it on the couch, then unfastened the dead man's kerchief and spread it over his face.

The door clicked. Hilda reappeared, her eyes red

from weeping, but the tears had stopped. She was plainly making an effort to control herself.

"Feeling better?" Terry asked quietly, and she gave a nod.

"Got over the first shock, anyhow. It's so—so *terrible*, Terry. I never suspected Dad would ever do a thing like that, no matter how tough things might be for him."

The informal use of his first name made Terry move forward. He put an arm about the girl's shoulders.

"I didn't get to know him very well in the short time I saw him," he said, "but he sure struck me as being the kind of character who'd stick anything out to the end."

"Evidently he wasn't," Hilda sighed. "That suicide confession shows that—"

"He puts the blame on me," Terry broke in. "But for my being here, you could have moved on," he said. "But that doesn't bear out what he told me last night. He told me then that he didn't move on because his roots were too deep. And there's something else. Why was his gun under the table?"

Interest began to kindle in Hilda's troubled eyes.

"Why?" Terry repeated with a grim glance. "Your father's body was some six feet away from the gun— in front of it. Are we to assume he wrote his confession, shot himself, and then threw the gun six feet away from him? He's been shot through the heart, Hil, and that means death would be instantaneous. The gun ought to have dropped right in front of him and him on top of it."

Hilda gave a bewildered look around her. "You—you mean that maybe he—he—"

"I mean I think he was murdered!"

"B-but who? Why?"

"At a rough guess, Sheriff Harrison. Why? In case he started talking too much to the one man who ought to be kept in the dark—myself."

Hilda sat down heavily at the table and spread her hands.

"I just don't understand, Terry."

"I'll explain," he said, his eyes glinting. "You've told me that you think Harrison had some kind of a hold on your father. The sheriff knew I intended staying around, and—to put it bluntly—poking my nose into things. Now, if your father knew something that was dangerous, it was possible he might pass on that information to me sometime. So the surest way to stop it was to kill him and make it look like suicide. The note was probably written at the point of a gun—and even in that a weak attempt is made to poison you against me, probably with the idea of sending me packing. Summed up briefly, I think this is a move of Harrison's in repayment for the way 1 kicked him out this morning."

"I suppose you could be right," Hilda said, thinking. "But what do you think Dad could have known that it might have been dangerous to pass on?"

"The answer to the four horsemen, perhaps," Terry responded. "He defended them with unnatural stubbornness every time they came into the conversation. You say you always suspected your Dad was getting short of money. One man who might have known that is Sheriff Harrison. Doesn't it occur to you, Hil, that your father may have been paid to keep his mouth shut about something? That would account for him wanting to leave, and yet not doing so. In other words, his natural inclinations were overpowered by the money he was being paid to keep quiet."

"It's all so terribly confused," Hilda said, shading her eyes.

"Not to me it isn't." Terry took out his gun and examined it critically before returning it to its holster; then he said: "I'm going right into town to see the sheriff, Hil. This so-called suicide has got to be reported, if only to cover the law. And at the same time I'm going to find out a few things on my own. I wouldn't advise you to come with me."

"I—I haven't the heart to," Hilda whispered. "I'll be glad to just sit here and try and get things straight in my mind. 1 guess you'd better advise Bill Carson, the blacksmith. He's the parson and undertaker around here."

"I'll do that," Terry promised. "And I'll be back as soon as I can."

CHAPTER THREE

Sheriff Harrison was enjoying a long, black cigar and reading a lurid-covered magazine when the door of his office flew open and was kicked shut again just as rapidly. He looked up with a scowl.

"Well, our ginger-headed stranger, huh?" he asked dryly, and tossed his magazine aside to survey Terry as he stood before him, thumbs latched in his pants belt.

"On your feet, Harrison," Terry ordered levelly.

"Huh? Who in hell are yuh talkin' to? Or have yuh forgotten I'm sheriff around here?"

"I'm forgettin' nothing, Harrison. The only thing that says you're a sheriff is that tin badge on your chest. I might be minded to knock it off. As far as law an' order goes, you don't know the first thing about it."

"Meanin' what?" Harrison demanded, glaring.

"Meaning Marchland!"

Harrison tightened his lips. He didn't like the steely glint in Terry's eyes.

"Marchland?" Harrison rubbed his stubbly jaw. "What 'bout the old critter?"

"Murdered. And I said get on your feet!"

Harrison obeyed, but at the same moment he whipped out his left-hand gun—and dropped it as Terry's fist crashed straight into his mouth and flung him helplessly against the desk. Blood trickling from his lip, Harrison stood glaring.

"I'm going to knock some information out of you, fella," Terry explained, kicking the fallen gun to a far corner of the little office. "I've reason for thinking you had something to do with Marchland being shot through the heart."

"Then you're loco," Harrison snarled.

"We'll see. I've a Colt here in my pocket with which Marchland was murdered. Out in this burg you mugs don't know much about fingerprint identification, but they do at police headquarters, and I'm banking on that." Terry remembered seeing an article about Sir Francis Galton's book, *Fingerprints*, and how it was bound to revolutionize criminal investigation. "I've taken care not to blur these gun prints, and I'm taking some of your prints as a sample. If they match, there will be a marshal down here to talk to you. Before I go I mean to get as much information from you as I can, starting right now."

On the last word Terry slammed out his right fist, and it hit Harrison clean in the stomach. He gulped, breath exploding from him, and for a moment his face purpled. Then he groaned as the fist struck him again like a pile-driver, flattening him amidst the papers on his desk. Hardly able to breathe, he struggled up and held his excruciating middle.

"What do you know about Marchland?" Terry asked deliberately.

"Nothin'! Yore a damned fool, Carlton! I don't know the first thing about—"

Harrison swung round and dropped flat on his face on the floor, hardly realising what had hit him. The blow, clean on the jaw, had half-paralysed him for a moment. Then he found himself hauled to his feet and slapped mercilessly back and forth across .the face until he thought his head would explode.

"Okay—okay," he whispered finally, his lips bleeding and one eye closing. "I'll—I'll start talkin'. It wus becos of Marchland that—"

Harrison got no further. The sudden deafening explosion of a gun from the slightly open window took care of him. He clapped a hand to his forehead, then lowered it again. Blood was trickling from a round hole in his skull. Pole-axed, he dropped to the floor.

Instantly, Terry whirled to the partly open window, slammed it up, and peered outside with his gun cocked. The assailant had disappeared. There were only one or two men and women on the boardwalk in the distance, certainly not near enough to have heard a shot. Terry compressed his lips, and drew the sash back into position. It was plain enough to him what had occurred. Somebody had been about to call on Harrison—somebody who counted in the whole mysterious set-up—and, noticing the open window, had looked in and realised that Harrison was about to shoot his face off.

So now what? Terry made a quick examination of

the sprawling sheriff and satisfied himself that he was dead. He pondered for a moment about taking some fingerprints, then decided against it. Even if they checked it wouldn't do any good with their owner in the grave. And, anyhow, it had only been intended partly as a scare to make Harrison talk.

Finally, he made his way to the door, peering around it cautiously on to the boardwalk in order to be sure nobody was I about to see him leave. The coast was reasonably clear, so he went further along the board-walk to Mayor Burridge's office and walked in.

The mayor of Verdure was a short, tubby little man with a genial grin and pink cheeks. Anybody could have liked him, but Terry was more wary. He remembered that Hilda had told him Burridge had a great deal of power in the town, and that didn't suggest he was lily-white.

"Morning, stranger," he greeted, looking up from the shiny I roll-top where he was working. "Something I can do for you?"

"Yeah." Terry sat down and noticed how neat and clean I the office was, compared to Harrison's. "I guess you can record two murdered men."

"I can?" Burridge looked startled. He had wide blue eyes, like those of a child awakened in the night. "That isn't my province, stranger. You should see the sheriff, further down the street."

"I did. He's one of the dead men."

Burridge swallowed hard. "Harrison—dead?"

"That's what I said." Terry was studying the man

intently, trying to make up his mind about him. "The other one is Marchland. You know him?"

"Sure do. Regular fella. So he's murdered, too?" Burridge's expression changed, and the grinning face became sinister. "How come you know so much about the business?"

"I'm staying with the Marchlands. When Miss Marchland and I got back from a ride this morning, we found old man Marchland shot through the heart. I went straight away for the sheriff and found him shot, too—through the head. Looks like there's a maniac or a trigger-happy outlaw on the loose somewheres. Only other person to report it to is you."

"Yeah, yeah, sure thing." Burridge looked troubled. "It is one hell of a shock to know 'bout Harrison. He was a good man."

"If you need a new sheriff, you haven't far to look," Terry said. "I'm not doing anything at present."

"I'll remember that," Burridge said. "First, though, I want a few facts about yourself—regarding your finding these two murders, I mean. How do I know but what you did 'em yourself?"

"You don't. But I didn't. That's all I aim to say. Best thing you can do if you want to check up is dig the slugs out of the bodies of both men and find the guns which match 'em. I know *this* gun is the one which killed Marchland—or, leastways, I think so."

Terry took the paper-wrapped Colt from his hip-pocket and laid it on the desk. The mayor looked at it, then glanced up.

"That's Marchland's *own* gun!" he snapped. "See that V-shaped piece bitten outa the butt there? I'd know it any place. Just what are you trying to pull, stranger?"

"I'm not trying to pull anything," Terry replied calmly. "I'm just showing you this gun because, legally, that's what I'm supposed to do. There are such things as fingerprint experts, remember—not around here, I don't mean, but in the big towns. They might find prints on this gun which would match Harrison's. And that'd be mighty interestin'."

"You don't mean you think *he* killed Marchland?"

"That's just what I mean." Terry put the Colt back in his pocket, then sat back in his chair and measured the mayor with steely eyes. "To hand it to you neat, mayor, I believe that you, the now dead Harrison, and a guy named Grant Swainson are running this town as you like—but to what exact end I'm not sure. I further think that Marchland was a man who knew too much, so he was rubbed out before he got too awkward."

"You've got your blasted gall, comin' in here accusin' me of such things. Get to hell outa here before I throw you out!"

Terry grinned a little. The idea of the fat little mayor throwing him out was fantastic.

"I'm going, anyway," Terry said. "Later on I'm tellin' the people of this town just what kind of a dirty set-up they're fighting, and I'll put them on their mettle to defeat it. So far, it seems they've been bouncin' around without anybody to lead 'em—so I'm taking it on. I might even get myself elected as sheriff—that's up to them. Right now, you're coming over to the Marchland place and take a look at that body before it's buried. That is, if you act as coroner around here."

"I don't!" Burridge retorted. "Bill Carson is the coroner, as well as blacksmith and parson."

"Okay, I'll get him. And I'm warning you, mayor, that if there is any more monkey business around this territory, you're going to get hurt—and those who work with you."

With that, Terry departed and went on his way to Bill Carson's forge. The massive blacksmith promptly accompanied him in a fancy buckboard to the Marchland home, took down all details concerning Marchland's body, then transferred it to the buckboard with the curt announcement that the funeral would be at ten the following morning. The crudity of it all, the contempt with which a dead body was treated, and the knowledge from Terry that the sheriff, too, was dead, left Hilda moodily silent.

Terry stood looking at her as the last rumbling of the funeral buckboard-hearse died away.

"What's done is done, Hil, I guess," he said at length, putting a hand on her shoulder. "Our job isn't to mope around because these damned thugs got your father; it's to blast their whole rotten plan wide open."

"*What* plan?" Hilda demanded, looking up in desperation. "What is it all *about*, Terry? That's what I can't understand! Phantom riders, my Dad murdered— and even the sheriff killed! Not that I'm worrying over that; but why was it so important that neither he nor

Dad should say too much?"

"Either of them might have given away the truth about the four phantom horsemen and blown a neat scheme sky-high," Terry said. "At least, that's my guess. I believe two other men know the truth, and they're still alive—Mayor Burridge and Grant Swainson. You said yourself that those two men, with Harrison, run the town."

"That's right, but—Terry, what are you going to do?"

"Become sheriff," he said, shrugging.

"But you can't—not just like that! It demands election, the mayor to swear you in. You don't suppose he'd ever do that, after the things you said to him, do you?"

"He may have no choice if the people want it. I'm going to put that to the test tonight."

"And Harrison? Who do you suppose murdered him?"

"Could have been the mayor—or mebbe Grant Swainson. If neither of them, then somebody who wanted Harrison shut up pronto. I might trace it from the bullet in Harrison—finding the gun to match— but that would expose me to too much danger, so I'm not risking it. I don't care much who killed Harrison, anyway; though, of course, the man responsible will have to be tried at some time."

There was a long silence. Terry sat down slowly on a chair so that he faced Hilda. She studied him through half-concealed tears.

"Just why are you taking all these risks?" she asked at last. "You're only a passer-through, Terry. Why get mixed up in such a dirty intrigue when you could just as easily ride off and leave it behind? You know as well as I do that, if they can, the powers-that-be in this town will try and pin the sheriff's murder on you, and probably the murder of Dad, too, since you have his gun."

Terry gave his infectious smile. "I'd thought of that, don't think they'll attempt that; deep down, they're afraid of me. They will be even more afraid if I'm elected sheriff. As to my staying on in Verdure— Well, I have you to protect, haven't I? You haven't a soul in the world who can stand by you now your Dad has gone."

"I—I appreciate that, Terry. I just don't know what *am* going to do henceforth."

"I'll tell you. You'll find out just how your affairs stand in the way of finance and so forth, and then you'll carry on living here as before. Whatever other time you have to spare you'll spend beside me, if you will."

"Nothing I'd like better. Trying to solve this mystery over the town, you mean?"

"Yeah. As for me, I'll have to move on, live someplace else. Now you're alone I can't stay. Unless—"

Hilda was silent, though she had a good idea what was coming.

"Bill Carson's the local preacher," Terry added. "D'you suppose you like me well enough to marry me, Hil? Then we can stick together, no matter what."

"I more than like you, Terry," she answered, her voice low. "Don't you remember me saying you're the only man I ever feel safe with around here? But do you think I should go to such lengths just to—?"

He took her in his arms and kissed her.

"I'm marrying you because I'm in love with you, Hil," Terry said tenderly, "and because it's the only decent way a man and woman can live together. And since you've taken me on trust, so to speak, you deserve to know more about me. You've already noticed that I've had a passable education. You're right. I come from a good family, only they stay put and I like to wander. Just one of those things. I like the open air and the trail. I couldn't get it way back in a city where I was learning to be an engineer. Ranching's more in my line."

"You don't have to explain yourself away," Hilda smiled.

"Okay. Just thought I'd explain. I came to Verdure by accident, because it happened to be in my track. Now I am here I'm sticking, chiefly because I think I've a self-appointed mission to accomplish in laying down this ghost business. What bit I've seen of this place so far convinces me it's being run by gun law— so I guess it's time I stepped in and showed certain gentlemen that they can't get away with it."

Hilda reflected. "Don't you think it might be more to the point to call in a marshal and have him look things over?"

"Might be—but even a marshal wouldn't do much without proof. I think we stand a better chance of working this out by ourselves. What I want to do is get proof of everything that seems phoney—then I could hand it over to the law and, with evidence before them, they could very soon go into action. Up to now, I haven't gotten far. I don't know how the four phantom horsemen do their vanishing act; I don't know who the men are behind it—not for certain; and I don't know why the scheme exists at all. Those things I have to find out. As things stand, I came into town as a lone rider, and I'm sticking. If I accomplished nothing else, I at least met you, and that's mighty good compensation."

Hilda smiled a little. "You certainly have the stuff in you to deal with this crooked set-up in Verdure, Terry," she said quietly.

"I think so." Terry got on his feet, hesitated, and then said: "I don't want to sound callous, Hil, but the living have to keep going. Both of us need a meal. Then this afternoon you'd better sort out your affairs, and this evening I'll try and shake the populace into making me sheriff. If that doesn't cause the mayor and other doubtful characters some discomfort, I'm crazy. At any rate, they'll see that I mean business—at gun point. Then, later, soon as can be considered decent, we'll be married."

* * * * * *

It was towards sunset when Terry and Hilda had their various affairs sorted out. Hilda had discovered that her father's bank account, becoming hers as next-of-kin at his death, was woefully small, but at least there was enough to last perhaps a year. The house was hers and one or two small-holdings of which she had

had no previous knowledge. Luckily her father had left a will, so there were no complications.

Terry for his part had spent most of the afternoon finding fresh lodgement and had finally settled for a room at the boarding house of Ma Granslade's in the main street.

So, for the time being, matters were as straight as they could be and the time for further action had come. Accordingly, towards, nine o'clock that same evening Terry and the girl arrived at the Black Coyote and entered it through the tightly fitting top-to-bottom doors.

Hilda coughed a little at the dense tobacco fumes which struck her. Terry stood looking about him, hand on his 45. It was surprising how busy the place really was, not one trace of which was evident from outside. Pretty nearly the whole population of Verdure seemed to be here, either at the bar or the tables. Some were busy with roulette in a far corner of the huge room, others were trying their luck at faro and poker. High up in the roof, swinging from massive beams, were the quadruple oil lamps which cast a yellow glow upon the proceedings.

"Couldn't be better," Terry murmured, taking the girl's arm. "I guess all the likely people to make me sheriff are here under one roof."

He moved forward, Hilda beside him. Men and women watched their progress towards the bar. Hilda was no stranger, even though she very rarely had visited the Black Coyote before; but Terry was something of a curiosity. News of his advent in town had already gone around the community.

At the bar-counter Terry stopped, ordering a whisky for himself and a sarsaparilla for Hilda, then he looked about him for a vacant table. The nearest one was occupied by two unshaven, grinning cowpunchers. Terry looked at them pensively for a moment.

"Feel like movin' on, fellas, to another table and make way for a lady?" he inquired easily, moving towards them.

They looked at each other, then the grins faded. "Who yuh tryin' to kid?" one of them demanded. "We've as much right to a durned table as you have! If you want one, yuh should come in time to get one."

"I said—for a lady," Terry repeated. "One thing you guys around here seem to lack is manners." His manner changed. "Blow!" he snapped.

Neither of the men made a movement. Terry knew what that meant. To back down on an order in a place like this would blackmark him forever. He glanced about him and noticed that everybody had become attentive, waiting to see what he would do. They saw—and mighty quickly.

Abruptly both Terry's hands lashed out and slammed at the back of each man's head. Their skulls crashed together with savage impact, and it brought them to their feet in fury. Without waiting a split second Terry whipped up his left arm and spun the first man off his feet with a haymaker to the jaw. The second man whipped out his gun, then he howled with pain as

Terry's own gun flashed with bewildering speed and drew blood. The puncher swore, his palm brimming, his gun on the floor.

"Now, move," Terry ordered, his eyes glinting. "Before I shoot the pants off you!"

The first man struggled up from the floor, cascading sawdust from his shirt and pants. He held his jaw, glared, then limped, away towards a further corner. The second man picked up his gun in his uninjured hand and holstered it, his eyes on the relentless barrel of Terry's .45.

When they had both gone to a safe distance, Terry relaxed, swept the beer glasses from the table with his hand and jerked up a chair. He motioned Hilda to it and, wide-eyed, she sat down. From the bar-counter Terry took the two drinks he had ordered and set them down on the table. Then he relaxed, his eyes darting about him warily.

Finally he found himself looking at a tall, thin man in a black suit standing at the bar, his black stetson at an angle on his dark hair. He came lounging forward.

"You'll be Carlton, I reckon?" he asked, and nodded to Hilda. "Howdy, Miss Marchland. Too bad about your father."

Terry looked at the man thoughtfully. He had a pleasant manner, a pretty smooth line of talk, and evidently knew his manners. He had raised his stetson when speaking to girl.

"This is Mr. Swainson," Hilda explained, seeing Terry's look. "He owns the place."

Terry nodded. "I've heard of you, Mr. Swainson—you've evidently heard of me."

"All I've heard of you is that you have been staying the Marchlands, so seeing you here—a stranger—with Miss Marchland, I guess I drew my own conclusions." Swainson mused for a moment, a smile on his powerful lips. "I liked the way you handled those two punchers," he added. "Pity there aren't more men around here with your spirit."

Terry glanced across at the distant corner where the two men he had hammered had taken refuge. They seemed to have forgotten all about the incident by now and were not even looking in his direction.

"I'm glad to see you aren't letting your father's—er—death get you down, Miss Marchland," Swainson added, and the girl gave him a quick look.

"I'm not in here just for the drink, Mr. Swainson, if that's what you're thinking! I've accompanied Ter—Mr. Carlton. He's got something to say to the folks."

"Yeah?" Swainson's dark eyes pinned Terry for a moment. "Like what?"

"I'll demonstrate," Terry told him and got to his feet—then onto the table. He called once for attention and didn't get it, so he fired his gun upwards twice in succession and brought an immediate halt in the conversation and din of the gaming tables.

"That's better," he said curtly, looking about him. "Folks, some of you know me; some of you don't. And I've got something to ask. How much longer are all of you goin' to be plumb scared of a phoney ghost story, even to the extent of some of you thinking of quitting town?"

The men and women looked at each other. One man stood up at the rear of the hall.

"There ain't no proof that them ghosts are phoney, stranger! I guess you ain't seen 'em or you wouldn't be talking this way!"

"I've seen 'em all right—last night, even to the extent of them vanishing in Star Canyon, but there were a lot of things about them that convinced me they're real flesh and blood. That being so, I figure it's time all of you came to your senses and opened up this town properly at night instead of cowering behind shutters."

The talking began again, urgently. Swainson settled himself in a chair, hands in his pants pockets and feet thrust out. No change of expression came to his lean face as he sat listening. Over in the distance Mayor Burridge got on his and made his way through the crowd.

"Yuh don't know what yore talkin' about, fella!" another man snapped. "Them ghosts is likely to come down into town any night—accordin' ter legend— an' set the whole caboodle afire. But if we keep the windows shuttered, lights off, like as not they'll figger there ain't anybody in town."

Terry stared in amazement for a moment, astounded any man could be so childish in his beliefs.

"You mean you think that keeping out of sight will do the trick?" he demanded.

"Sure thing!" a woman said fiercely. "Mayor

Burridge and the sheriff both told us that, and they're men who ought to know."

"Ought to, but don't," Terry retorted. "I guess you all musta heard by now that the sheriff was killed today by a bullet through his brain. If he couldn't take care of himself, how d'you expect he could have taken care of you? You're nothing but a lot of sheep," he added bitterly. "Whole durned lot of you!"

There was no resentment, just an obstinate shaking of heads.

"Ghosts ain't things ter argue with, fella," a man snapped.

"These are *not* ghosts!" Terry declared flatly. "And if some of you would have the nerve to stay beside me and investigate this business, we'd darned soon prove there no ghosts! You can't see it, but you're all being kicked outa town as part of a plan. Somebody wants this territory bad, and to get it without paying for it yore bein' spoon-fed a ghost story. Harrison knew the facts and got shot before he could tell 'em. Marchland also was mixed up in it, and he too got rubbed out before he could talk too much."

"How do you know all this?" Mayor Burridge demanded, coming to the front. Then before Terry could answer he swung on the people about him and added: "I believe this guy is the killer himself, but I can't prove it. If you folks want to listen to him you—"

"Oh, let the guy talk," Swainson broke in, in his easy voice. "He's interesting even if he is crazy."

"Crazy, huh?" Terry gave a hard smile. "Listen,

folks, tell me how crazy this is: I found Marchland murdered this morning after he had received a visit from the sheriff, during which visit I threw the sheriff off the premises. In other words the sheriff was aware that I intended to sift this ghost business to the bottom. I believe he killed Marchland to stop him having too much conversation with me. Next thing I went to the sheriff to report the death of Marchland, then, when I'd gotten him to the point where he was willing to confess the whole truth, ghost riders included, he was shot dead. Somebody must have heard him—somebody who was maybe going to call on the sheriff an' saw us through the window. Two people have died today because they knew the facts about this campaign to drive you good folks out of town."

"I tell you this man's a liar," Burridge half shouted. "He's making all this up to cover his own guilt!"

"If I'd shot those two men, mayor, I'd have hit the trail long ago," Terry told him. "And you know it!"

"Just how much good was Harrison to us?" Hilda asked suddenly, getting to her feet and thumping the table. "When these ghosts were first seen, we told him about them. He rode out with a posse and came back with the story that nothing could be done. Instead he issued an order, in conjunction with the mayor here, that we were to barricade ourselves in at night! I believe, as Mr. Carlton does, that the whole phantom affair is a scare. We're going to be literally frightened away from our homes."

"But why?" asked Swainson, puzzling, "What good

would it be? There's nothing valuable on this land—far as I know. What do you say, mayor?"

"Sure isn't," Burridge agreed, with a black glance in Terry's direction.

"What we need is a sheriff who'll look after our interests—who'll tear this whole intrigue up by the roots," Hilda insisted. "I'm one of you; I've suffered more than any of you because I've lost my father. I think Mr. Carlton should take Harrison's place as sheriff."

"A killer as sheriff?" Burridge roared. "Like hell!"

"Take that back, mayor," Terry flashed at him, his gun in his hand. "I'm about tired of you calling me a murderer without ever trying to prove it! I could call *you* one, I guess, only I won't till I'm sure."

"Me? I never killed anybody in my life! An' I still say that if anybody killed Harrison, it was you—to get his daughter!"

Terry fired. Burridge gave a yell as he felt hot hell sear over the top of his head. He did not know why he was alive—then he realised his hat had been blown clean off. A puncher handed it to him with a dry grin.

"Any more cracks, mayor?" Terry demanded. "For every one you make, I'll remove a button from that fancy waistcoat of yours—granting you stand sideways, otherwise you're likely to get the slugs clean in that overfed belly."

"The guy can shoot," somebody said, with approval.

"Yeah—so can I," snapped a man at the back, and Terry was just in time to see one of the two men he had man-handled leap up with a gun in his bandaged hand.

Terry fired with split-second timing. For the second time that evening the gun-hawk found himself defenceless and already wounded hand turned red in its bandage.

"Sorry, fella," Terry shouted at him. "You asked for it."

There was a grim silence. Then Burridge shouted: "I protest! A guy like this for a sheriff would—"

"Be just the guy!" yelled a bearded rancher, leaping up. "I reckon the fella talks our language. He can handle a gun, ain't afraid to speak up and even put the mayor in his place if he feels inclined. I'm for him! There never has bin a guy around here who acted like he was a real sheriff."

"Yeah—you said it."

"Seems to me the issue's settled itself, Carlton," Swainson said, getting to his feet. "The folks seem to want you fer sheriff, and I sure agree we need one. Can't think of anybody more suitable for the job, 'less mebbe myself—and I've enough on my hands running this place."

Terry said nothing. He was wondering for a moment if his preconceived notion of Swainson had been wrong. If he was really on the level after all.

"Only thing we can do is vote on it," Swainson said. "I second Miss Marchland's proposal that you should be elected as sheriff. How many of you folks here are in favour?"

Well over three-quarters of the people in the big room raised their hands. Swainson gave a nod.

"That settles it," he said. "Swear him in, mayor."

"Are you loco, Swainson?" Burridge demanded, coming forward.

"I said swear him in." The saloon owner spoke deliberately. "Then afterwards it's drinks all round and a plan of campaign. I'll be mighty glad to get the shutters down and breathe fresh air in the joint at night."

Mayof Burridge just gazed. He seemed incapable of realising what had happened.

CHAPTER FOUR

It was close on midnight when Terry prepared to take his farewell of Hilda. They had walked slowly from the closed Black Coyote and were standing outside the front gate of her home. The deathly quiet of the shuttered town was around them.

"You got your wish," Hilda muttered. "They made you sheriff, though I can't understand why Swainson came to your side. I'm still sure he's no good, any more than Burridge."

Terry smiled in the dim light. "A clever man plays the enemy as well as the friend," he answered. "I learned that long ago. He has more brains than that fool Burridge. I shall become particularly wary of Swainson from here on. Perhaps he figgers he can lead me into a trap someplace. Anyway, as things stand, we set off tomorrow night to comb Star Valley. We'll be on the spot if the four horsemen appear. If they don't, all the better. There's just a chance that knowing we'll be ready for action, Swainson or Burridge—if they are mixed up in it—will call a halt until they decide how to get me out of the way."

"I shan't have an easy moment whenever you're

away from me," Hilda said.

"Cuts both ways, Hil. But there are some conventions we've got to observe, I'm afraid. Sort it out properly when we've buried your Dad tomorrow morning. 'Bye for now; try not to worry."

Terry kissed her gently and then turned away, heading back up the street to Ma Granslade's apartment house. Hilda watched him go and then turned moodily into the garden, began walking slowly up the pathway to the porch steps.

She could not explain why, but just at that moment some instinct made her glance behind her. She was just in time to see a dark shape at the gateway advancing towards her. The figure stopped as she turned, and something thwacked hard into the pillar of the porch. Then the figure was rushing away into the street without waiting to see the result of his handiwork.

Hilda looked at the pillar intently, and then gave a start as she saw a thin-bladed knife still swinging gently by its point. The blade was transfixing a folded note. A little shakily, she pulled the knife free and removed the note gingerly. Entering the hall, she lighted the oil lamp and read quickly:

THIS DEAD BODY IS TO WARN YOU, CARLTON, TO GET OUT OF VERDURE WHILST YOU ARE SAFE. NEXT TIME IT WILL BE YOU.

It only occurred to Hilda then how near she had been to death. The note had been written in the belief that she would be killed. Maybe she would have been, too, had she not glanced round and caused her potential killer to fling his knife and run for it rather than risk identification.

Hilda made up her mind immediately. Her nerve had gone for the time being. She couldn't stay alone in the house all night with such danger stalking her. So she left the house quickly and hurried out to the street. It seemed deserted enough. She risked it, and arrived without mishap at Ma Granslade's boarding-house five minutes later. The old girl grumbled at being aroused after midnight, but nonetheless showed the distraught girl to Terry's room on the top floor. Apparently he had not gone to bed, for he opened the door immediately.

"Hil, he exclaimed in surprise, as she stood in the light of the lamp Ma Granslade was holding.

"I ain't sayin' I approve uv this sorta thing," Ma said grimly, "but the gal seemed so distressed I figgered yuh'd better see her."

"I need a room for the night—after I've spoken with Mr. Carlton," Hilda said urgently. "You've just got to fix me up, Ma!"

"Well, okay." Ma rubbed her chin. "Second door, next floor down. We'll square up in the mornin'. I'm missin' my sleep!"

She went on her way, and Terry held the door wider. Hilda entered and sank down thankfully in the solitary armchair.

"What gives?" Terry asked, turning from lighting the oil lamp on the dresser.

"This." Hilda handed him the knife and note and briefly explained the circumstances. He frowned as he listened, then he took the knife over to the lamp and examined it carefully. "Indian knife," he said. "Nothing very special about it to give us a clue as to the owner. And you saw somebody throw it at you?"

"A man, Terry. I couldn't make out his features. He seemed medium-sized and was wearing a sombrero. There's no doubt he intended to stab me in the back, but I turned before he could do it. So he threw the knife instead. I suppose, in case he missed, he didn't want me to recognise him."

"Uh-huh." Terry was examining the note carefully, both under and before the oil-flame. "Pretty good throwing, too, with a note fixed on to it," he commented.

"Looks like the first move to get rid of you now you've been made sheriff," Hilda added. "Striking at you through me, that is. Whoever killed Dad and the sheriff evidently is making an effort to kill me too."

"Yeah. Seems pretty certain, from the wording of the note, that your being killed was a foregone conclusion. This note is on fair quality paper, and written with a good pen. Not the kind of thing you'd find an ordinary puncher or maybe a disgruntled Redskin using. There is also education in the wording—the word 'whilst' being but one sample."

"Burridge or Swainson!" Hilda exclaimed. "They're both men of passable education."

"Right! And mebbe one of them has been a bit too smart in throwing this into the enemy camp. If I can prove where the ink and paper came from, I can probably fit in the rest. It's pieces of evidence like this that I need."

"It was neither Burridge nor Swainson who threw the knife at me," Hilda said, reflecting. "I'd know their figures."

"Hardly would be. And a knife was used so no bullets could be traced and so no sound would be heard if anybody was awake near your home. Best thing I can do is forego my sleep for a while and take a look round the abodes of both Burridge and Swainson. I want to find a paper and ink similar to these we have here."

His mind made up, Terry took the knife across to a drawer in the dresser. He put it beside the still paper-wrapped gun with which old man Marchland had been killed.

"Exhibits," he explained, closing the drawer and turning. "I guess they'll be useful if certain gentlemen are brought to trial later on. Right now, Hil, you'd better get along to your room on the floor below and leave the rest to me."

Hilda nodded and got to her feet. Terry accompanied her below, then went on his way to the outdoors. He left the building quietly and kept well to the shadows as he advanced down the main street to the big white dwelling which Hilda had pointed out earlier as the abode of Burridge.

Gun in hand, Terry sped across the flowerbeds in the back garden until he came to the usual French-type of window belonging to the living room. To deflect the catch with his penknife blade was only the work of a moment; then he glided into the dark interior. For a long time he stood listening, and heard no sounds.

Satisfied, he pulled over the window drapes tightly and felt round for the oil-lamp on the table. Lighting it at a low glimmer, he looked about him, then went over to the open bureau in the corner. Five minutes searching was enough to prove to him that there was no paper resembling that dispatched with the dagger.

"Wrong angle, mebbe," he muttered. "Perhaps paper which he uses in his office. Else Swainson's back of it—"

He stopped suddenly. A bundle of papers with a tape round it had caught his eye. It was the tail end of a word— '…hland'—which attracted him. He drew the paper out and studied it carefully. The paper was executed in the form of an invoice, referring to the sum of $3,000 having been paid to Joseph Marchland in return for the transfer of 1,000 head of cattle. What was even more interesting was the fact that Marchland's signature, acknowledging the money, was sprawled at the bottom of the sheet.

Terry thought for a moment, and then stuffed the paper in his shirt pocket. He searched further, with meticulous thoroughness, and came upon two more similar invoices. Since this seemed to be the limit, he added them to the one he already had, tidied the bureau up again, then blew out the lamp and departed.

He had not found the identifying paper he was seeking, but had instead discovered something that might be just as useful. It all depended whether the cattle referred to in the invoices were 'straight' or 'rustled'. If the latter variety, then a good deal of the mystery which had surrounded Marchland might be a mystery no longer.

Still pursuing his original objective, Terry went next to the mayor's office and forced his way in, to discover a locked roll-top and an impregnable safe. Rather than leave signs of his activity by smashing open the desk, he retired again and instead went on to the Black Coyote. Here he was beaten. Heavy bars over the window of Swainson's office defeated him—and the front doors of the saloon were so heavily secured he just could not make any impression on them without a crowbar.

Pondering, he stood in the shadows of the board-walk and looked over the moonlit town. He was in the midst of debating whether he ought to ride out to Swainson's spread and investigate when he realised the sound of an approaching horseman was echoing on the still air. Immediately he drew his gun and moved well back into gloom cast by the bulk of the Black Coyote.

In a matter of minutes, the horseman became visible, riding hard from the direction of the desert trail—or so Terry assumed at first. Then he noticed that the horseman was not sitting upright in the saddle, but was half-lying on the creature's neck—either dead, asleep, or somehow incapable.

It took Terry a split second to make up his mind. He hurtled out of concealment, vaulted the tie-rail at the side of the boardwalk, then dived across to the runaway. In a matter of seconds, he had dragged the snorting animal to a standstill and pulled down the barely conscious rider into the dust.

The man stirred weakly, and Terry watched him, gun ready. He gave a start as he saw the man had one hand bandaged.

"You, huh?" he asked briefly, as the moonlight caught the man's features. "The guy I shot twice in the Black Coyote tonight?"

"Yeah," the puncher whispered. "Guess I've— I've packed more lead since then. That dirty skunk Swainson—"

He broke off, coughing thickly. Dark stain came to his lips.

"What gives?" Terry asked quickly, kneeling beside him. "How come you're ridin' with a slug in your lungs? What's this about Swainson?"

"I—I—had ter tell him I—I weren't sure if I got the dame or not—an' jus' fur that he put a bullet in me, then sent me ridin'."

"Dame? You mean Hilda Marchland?"

"Yeah." The puncher breathed hard. It was clear he had not got long. "Ter-night Swainson gave me a note—an' a knife. He told me ter watch fur you an' the gal leaving the Coyote. I was t'get the gal fust—then later mebbe get you, I was more'n willin', I guess, after th' way yuh'd shot at me. Only the gal looked round an' saw me. I wasn't takin'—"

"I know," Terry interrupted. "You threw the knife and ran for it. Miss Marchland isn't hurt. Then what?

You reported to Swainson?"

"Sure—at his spread. He shot me fur not doin' my job properly, shoved me on my cayuse, and sent it packin'. It just followed the trail, comin' right back inter town here. I guess Swainson didn't care where it went. He knew he'd got me an' that I'd drop somewheres dead. I—I guess he wus right, too. I'm all in, Carlton."

"You're not so all in you can't sign a statement before you die," Terry snapped. "I want evidence of what you did, that you obeyed Swainson's orders."

The puncher said nothing. He lay breathing hard in the cold moonlight whilst Terry scribbled busily on a crumpled sheet of paper from his hip pocket. Finally, he hauled up the puncher's head and shoulders and put the pencil in his hand.

"Sign it," he ordered; and, too weak to argue the point, the puncher obeyed. The dim signature of 'Al Naycross' became visible.

"I—I hope this gets Swainson in mighty bad," he whispered. "He—he's got it comin'—"

"What else do you know about Swainson?" Terry demanded. "Is he mixed up in some kind of cattle rustling and connected with the four phantom horsemen?"

He found he was talking to himself. The puncher had relaxed, his eyes fixed on the night sky. Terry shrugged to himself and hauled the body up, dumping it on the horse. He led the animal down the main street, halting it when he arrived outside the home of Bill Carson, the blacksmith. After a while Carson appeared, flinging open the screen door impatiently.

"What the devil d'yuh—" Then he broke off, his tone changing. "Oh, it's you, Sheriff. What gives, this hour uv night?"

"The hour of night doesn't matter if you're a public servant," Terry told him. "Here's a body for burial—Al Naycross by name. Murdered. I got the particulars from him before he died. The rest of the job's up to you; his horse you can take for auction in the livery market. Okay?"

"Okay," Carson agreed, and hauled the corpse from the saddle. "Murdered, you say? Who?"

"That's my worry. Just get on with your job and I'll get on with mine. Let me have your certificate when the body's been buried."

With that Terry departed, satisfied that the legal side had been taken care of; but he did not set off for Swainson's ranch and attempt to arrest him. Instead, he returned to Ma Granslade's and went to bed. Sleep was essential if he were ever to keep alert; and it proved to be a long sleep, too. It was past nine in the morning when he awoke to the glare of the sun.

He shaved and dressed hurriedly, and then went down to breakfast. Hilda was the only other person present; everybody else had finished, which fact Ma Granslade herself wasn't slow to mention.

"I've reg'lar hours fur my boarders," she said, when she had put Terry's breakfast before him. "I'd be obliged if yuh'i keep to 'em, sheriff or no sheriff."

"Okay, Ma," Terry assured her, smiling. "I had some

night work to do; guess I overslept."

Ma muttered something and then went out. Immediately, Hilda gave Terry an anxious look.

"How did you get on during the night?"

"Well enough. I got plenty of evidence, and ran into a murder as well."

"*Another* murder?"

Terry gave the details as he ate his breakfast. He had finished it by the time his story was over, and Hilda carefully examined the invoices he handed to her. Her frown deepened after a while.

"From the look of these," she said, "Dad was in receipt of about three thousand dollars every time he signed one of these invoices. What do you suppose became of the money? There was hardly anything in his account at the bank."

"I can only hit in the dark," Terry answered seriously. "My guess is that your Dad was a go-between between Burridge and some other party. There's nothing there to show that the cattle deals were not legitimate, but I think that perhaps some gang has been stealing cattle—not necessarily in this territory—and passing them on to Burridge, your father acting as the medium between. As to the money, it doesn't say that money was all your *father's*; it may have been the amount paid to the thieves, for which your father was responsible. Probably he drew an agent's percentage."

"You refer only to Burridge, Terry? What about Swainson? Since it was he who tipped off that puncher last night to kill me, I suppose he's mixed up in it, too?"

"Sure he is, but he's smart enough to keep his name off any papers. I always said Burridge was a dimwit. I think Swainson is using him as a cat's-paw."

Terry took the notes back and considered. "That," he said, "is how things look. Later we may confront Burridge or Swainson with this evidence and see how they wriggle. I'm expecting something to happen mighty fast when Burridge finds these invoices gone from his desk."

"It's part of the problem solved, perhaps," Hilda said, thinking, "but it still doesn't explain the ghost horsemen or the reason for them."

"Sure it doesn't?" Terry asked dryly.

"Well, I—I can't see the connection. If cattle rustling is at the back of everything, what possible relation can it have to trying to scare away the populace?"

"The answer's so simple I wonder I didn't think of it before," Terry said. "This town is called Verdure on account of its wonderful pasturelands, the best for miles around. Now, supposing Swainson, Burridge, and mebbe others have a whole flock of stolen cattle some-where and need good pastures to fatten them before selling? What better place to feed them than right in this territory? But how can they do it unless everybody is scared right out of town—except, of course, those who know what's going on."

Hilda snapped her fingers. "You've got it, Terry!"

"I think I have. And the longer the delay in scaring everybody out of town, the more the stolen cattle will suffer. They must have the best grazing land if they are to be worth selling. Since they're hidden somewhere, they can't be enjoying life at the moment. From here on, since last night, I told everybody to stay put and fight. Swainson, Burridge, and others may try everything they can to be rid of me and those who support me—you included."

"And the cattle? Where do you think they might be?"

"I dunno. Star Canyon perhaps. Anyway, I'm convinced those four horsemen are purely a means to an end. Of course, I've no proof as yet that the cattle referred to have *been* stolen, but it seems mighty likely."

"Can't have been stolen from any ranches about here," Hilda said, "or we'd have heard about it. And what about Swainson?" she added quickly. "Now you have proof that he ordered Al Naycross to knife me, and afterwards shot him because he bungled it, aren't you going to arrest him?"

Terry shook his head. "That wouldn't be good policy. With him arrested, the mainspring might fall out of the plan aimed against this territory, and we'd never solve it. It would also let a lot of smaller fish go free. Best thing is to let him carry on, unaware that I know the facts. He'll hear about Naycross being buried, of course, and that he was murdered—but he won't know I'm aware of the killer's identity." Terry got to his feet, and Hilda, her meal finished, did likewise.

"We've Dad's funeral to attend," she said quietly. "You haven't forgotten?"

"Nope. I'm coming home with you while you change into black. I don't trust you being left by yourself after last night."

They left the rooming-house together and returned down the main street to the girl's dwelling. Whilst she disappeared into her bedroom to don black, Terry did what he could with a piece of black cloth round his shirt sleeve.

When he saw her again he was surprised how little black suited her. The crinoline-style dress and poke bonnet with ribbons under the chin made her look ten years older.

"This was mother's," she explained. "I kept it back against a time like this when I might have to use it."

Terry nodded, but he said nothing. He took the girl's arm, and they went down the front path. From the gate to the graveyard at the back of the tabernacle on the outskirts of the town it was only ten minutes' walk. Such a thing as a funeral procession was unknown in this region. One dead body more or less meant nothing, just as long as the last rites were performed.

Most of the people of Verdure seemed to be present round the oblong grave Bill Carson had prepared. Whilst he gave the short funeral service from a worn Bible, Terry glanced about him. He noticed that Mayor Burridge and Swainson were both present, their hats off, both looking very solemn. It made Terry writhe inwardly that they could have such gall; then it occurred to him that as prominent citizens there was little else they could do but attend. Marchland had been a pretty respected man in the district.

Throughout the proceedings Hilda kept her face

averted, and when the crude coffin was lowered into the earth, she turned away. Terry followed slowly after her as she went down the churchyard. He had just caught up with her when an unfamiliar voice spoke.

"You're the sheriff around here, ain't you, sir?" Terry turned in surprise. A burly, middle-aged man, travel-stained, red-faced, was advancing towards him.

"That's right," Terry assented, nodding to the star-badge on his shirt. "Anything wrong, stranger?"

"You won't know me—I'm from Winslow way. I took the stage specially to have a word with th' sheriff of this burg. You busy right now?"

"Not now." Terry glanced towards the assembly moving from Marchland's grave. "We've been burying this young lady's father—he was the victim of a killer."

"Mighty bad," the stranger sympathised, as Hilda gave a wan glance. "I figgered somethin' important must be goin' on 'cos I couldn't find anybody when I rode inter town. Anyways, can we go to your office, sheriff?"

"Sure thing—an' you'd better go back to Ma Granslade's, Hil, and wait for me."

"I'll come with you that far," she said. "Be safer."

The stranger gave a mystified look but didn't ask any questions. Nor did he say anything until he and Terry were behind the closed door of the sheriff's office.

"It's about stolen cattle," the stranger said. "My name is Art M'Cord, and I run the Twelve-K spread near Winslow. Around my territory there's mebbe twenty other spreads, each havin' some of the biggest corrals an' best cattle yuh could wish t'see. Leastways they *did*, until some Dad-blamed bandits recently started to do some thievin'."

"Carry on," Terry invited, listening attentively.

"These stealings have bin going on now fur about three months. All of us have lost a good deal of cattle. We got the sheriff to get together a posse an' we started searchin'—but we couldn't find them blamed steers anywheres. But we *did* find some trails, and they come straight in this direction—or at least towards yonder mountains. We had a pow-wow to see what could be done, an' finally I got meself delegated to make inquiry down here. It's the nearest town to the mountain range, an' it looks like you might be able t'help with some information."

"Have you any idea of the exact number of cattle stolen?" Terry asked.

M'Cord rubbed his big chin. "Not exactly. All I can say is there's a helluva lot of 'em. I can't rightly figger how anybody could keep that number uv steers outa sight."

"Obviously they can," Terry replied, musing. "Later, all that will be necessary will be to change the brands, or burn them off entirely, and that will be that. I'm glad you came to inquire, M'Cord. You've helped me more than you realise."

"Y'mean you have an idea where them cattle might be?"

"Not right now, but I've a notion who's back of them being stolen. Best thing you can do is return home and mount guard all round your territory. Get a permit from your sheriff to shoot on sight if you find any thieving—and leave me to sort the rest out from here. The moment I've some definite news about your cattle I'll contact you, either direct or through your sheriff."

"Good enough for me," M'Cord said, satisfied. "Yuh look like a guy who knows his job. Well, I guess I'll grab meself some food and a rest and then be gettin' back home. Mighty nice t'have met yuh, Mr. Carlton."

Terry shook hands, and then stood thinking when M'Cord had gone. He looked about the office for a while. It had only just occurred to him that this was the first time he had occupied it in an official capacity; but he had little doubt that everything in the nature of evidence to help his cause had been removed long since, either by Burridge or Swainson.

There was a sudden sound at the office door. Terry came back from preoccupation and found himself looking at Swainson. His thin face was smiling deceptively.

"Gettin' bedded in?" he inquired, looking about him.

"Uh-huh." Terry waited for the next, an eyebrow raised.

"Just wonderin' about tonight," Swainson added, resting an elbow on the roll-top. "Are we still keeping to the plan we mapped out—to set a watch on Star Canyon?"

Terry shook his head. "No, I've changed my mind. I want to work out a different strategy. I'd intended telling you later to cancel tonight; since you've looked in that's saved me the trouble."

"Yeah." Swainson seemed to be having difficulty in not looking surprised. "What do you aim to do, then? Let these phantom raiders do as they like if they show up?"

Terry gave a grim smile. "If we're on the look-out for them, Swainson, they *won't* show up. They're controlled by somebody—or a group of men—in this town. Those men know right now we had intended going tonight to waylay the spooks—so naturally they'll call the whole thing off."

"Could be," Swainson agreed, without moving a muscle. "Which means they've a better chance of showing up if we don't watch for them?"

"Right. Tell everybody else concerned that that plan is off. I'm going to work out a different strategy. Soon as I've done it I'll tip you off."

Swainson took his elbow from the roll-top and considered; then he asked a casual question: "Who was the big stranger who came to see you?"

"Private business, Swainson. You're not entitled to know."

"Okay, don't get sore—and don't get too big for your boots, either. No sheriff lasts long around here if he don't play the game the way it should be played. Anyway, I've a reason for coming here. I could have mentioned it at the graveyard, only it wasn't a good moment with so many mourners around. I'm reporting a theft on behalf of Mayor Burridge."

"Yeah?" Terry's eyes narrowed. "Is Mayor Burridge incapable of telling me himself?"

"Nope, but I happened to be coming this way to my saloon and he wasn't. He's had some cattle consignment bills stolen—sometime during the night. Signs of the window in his living room having been broken into. He figgered you might look into it—as sheriff."

"Mebbe I will," Terry agreed. "I've two other jobs on first, though. The murder of Al Naycross and the attempted murder of Miss Marchland. I guess they have first call on my time."

Swainson hesitated, then he shrugged. He was still poker-faced.

"Okay, up to you. All I'm doing is reporting. Let me know when you've gotten that new strategy worked out."

With a nod, he turned and left the office. Not very long after him, Terry departed too, and went over to Ma Granslade's. He found Hilda quite safe in the big living room, apparently waiting for him to show up.

"I got worried," she said. "I've been watching through the window, and I saw first that big fellow who wanted to talk to you leaving, and then Swainson. I wondered if between them—"

"There's no connection between them, Hil," Terry interrupted. "I gathered enough from the stranger—M'Cord by name—that the cattle we're wondering about *were* stolen, and as far as Swainson is concerned, I've laid a trap."

"How—a trap?"

Terry filled in the details and then explained: "I've called off the Star Canyon hunt tonight on purpose. We'd have wasted our time. If Swainson or Burridge are back of the phantoms, they naturally would lie low, knowing an attack was pending. Now I've called it off, it is possible the phantoms will appear. If they do, that satisfies me that it's Swainson or Burridge who are back of them."

"Yes, but what do we do? Sit still and wait?"

"No. We watch Star Canyon on our own account, just you and I, and this time we'll see if we can't solve the riddle of where those horsemen go to. Once we've got that, we've probably got the key as to where the cattle have been hidden. Right now we'll go back to your place and stay there until evening—unless you think we could better occupy the time by getting married?"

Hilda hesitated, so Terry developed the situation quickly. "Your father's buried now, Hil; it can't make much difference whether we marry now or next year. I think it should be as soon as possible if I'm to protect you adequately."

"Very well," Hilda agreed quietly. "I suppose it is the most sensible course—but give me time to find something a little less drab than this dress."

"Come along back home and take your time finding something," Terry suggested, taking her arm.

CHAPTER FIVE

By four o'clock in the afternoon Terry and Hilda were man and wife. They both retained black bands about their arms, in respect to Marchland, but otherwise they were grimly determined to go on with the business of living, both feeling more secure now they had the legal right to live side by side.

They had no celebration meal, no anything. They were thinking of nightfall and a job that had to be done. Both of them had the instinctive feeling that the calm in which they were at present existing would explode any minute. Neither had any illusions about the fact that Swainson, or Burridge—or both—would make a definite move before long, in case their own plans were thrown into confusion.

Towards sunset Terry left the house with Hilda beside him. Ostensibly they went to pay up Ma Granslade—and Terry to get his horse—but actually their aim was to see if anything seemed to be stirring in the town itself. Apparently nothing was. The twilight gloom was upon it, and the shutters were being put up to the windows.

"Do you suppose anybody will say anything with

you not having been in your office today?" Hilda asked, as they walked back home with Smoky behind them.

"Let them," Terry shrugged. "As long as I'm sheriff, I'll go where I wish and do as I choose."

So Hilda said no more. Since Terry seemed to know what he was doing, there was no reason why she should worry—but she did just the same. She moved about with the constant feeling that a knife would suddenly flick from somewhere, or a bullet would be fired, meant either for her or Terry.

She was thankful when they gained the comparative safety of home again. There was nothing to do now but wait for darkness to completely fall; then they could be off under the friendly cover of the night sky.

As the light faded, Terry stood by the window, checking his gun and the cartridge bandolier about his waist. Beside him, Hilda was doing likewise. She was dressed ready for action in her divided skirt, blouse, and leather mackinaw, the floral kerchief wound about her head.

"Two against—how many?" she asked, thinking. "Ever stop to consider the odds, Terry?"

"No; wouldn't do my nerve any good. All I realise is that when we solve the mystery of the four horsemen and find those stolen cattle, we'll have the whole business in the bag. I can act then, put the evidence before the authorities, and the necessary arrests can be made."

"You've got that far then?"

"Obviously. I have written proof from the dead Al Naycross concerning Swainson; I've invoices about the implication of your father and Burridge; I've the knife with which an attempt was made to kill you—which can be proved to be Swainson's property; and I have the gun which killed your father. I think Harrison killed him. In any case, prints can be taken from his exhumed body, and checked with those on the gun."

"I never thought you'd gathered so much," Hilda mused.

"But the worst has yet to come," Terry reminded her grimly. "Swainson and Burridge know full well that I'm dangerous, and we can expect just anything from them. Our only hope is to be quicker than they are."

He paused and looked out of the window, as with characteristic abruptness the twilight vanished and the night came. He glanced at the girl in the gloom.

"Ready, Hil?"

She nodded and moved away. Terry spent a moment making sure the small safe was locked—in which was all the evidence he had gathered so far—then he followed the girl outside to the waiting horses. They left by the rear double-gate and cantered slowly across the starlit pasture land, the night wind blowing in their faces.

Before long, they had drawn away from the town, and, by a detour, reached the trail which led to the mountain foothills. But they did not stay on it for long. Terry changed direction suddenly, so that they were parallel with the trail but moving through the long grass behind the tall hedge skirting it.

"Just in case tabs are being kept on our movements—as they probably are," he explained. "We don't want to be seen on the actual trail—giving away our possible destination— What's that?" he broke off, halting abruptly.

Hilda drew up too, listening to the sound of approaching hoofs.

"We're being followed," she said hoarsely. "That must be it—"

"Coming the other way," Terry corrected. "From the mountains, not the town—"

Then again he stopped speaking. Words had become suddenly useless before the awe-inspiring vision of four phantom horsemen, white as snow, speeding with rhythmic precision down the trail, heading towards the town. They were moving fast, too, two in front and two behind, keeping an exact distance, just as though they were controlled by clockwork.

"They—they never came this way before!" Hilda gasped, her eyes fixed on them as they passed close to where she and Terry were mounted, watching, but almost concealed by the tall hedge.

"Apparently they mean business," Terry snapped. "Heading towards Verdure can mean trouble. Quick, after 'em!"

He wheeled his horse round and dug in the spurs, sending the animal pelting through the long grass. It kept him on a line with the trail without actually touching it, and thereby becoming visible against its whiteness, but it also meant he was slowed up. The horse could not move as swiftly on grass, rank and tangled, as on baked earth.

Gradually the speeding phantom horsemen became less distinct as distance increased.

"Damn!" Terry swore, as Hilda came up beside him. "I'm right out of gun-range. I was going to shoot and chance it, see if it brought one of them down. Anyway, if I can't hit them, they can't hit us. Let's get onto the trail." He swung his horse's head and plunged from the top of the bank to the bottom, then he whipped the animal's withers fiercely and sent him tearing onwards into the starlight, pursuing the now remote four white specks. Hard though he rode, Terry did not catch up, and long before he reached Verdure he had ample evidence of the phantoms' intentions. One of them seemed abruptly to catch fire when he reached the main street, then it became apparent a moment later that he was whirling a lighted torch. It sailed through the air and landed on top of one of the dwellings. Another followed it from one of the other horsemen: after that the thing was done.

The horsemen sped onwards, never pausing a moment, but they had left behind them a rapidly growing conflagration which, in a tinder-dry town, could not help but reduce it to ashes in the space of perhaps an hour.

"What now?" Hilda asked urgently, her eyes on the gathering blaze as they hurtled nearer to it.

"Ride straight on," Terry answered. "Shout 'Fire!' as we go and leave it to the folks to deal with: we're going after those horsemen whilst we're still on their track."

Hilda nodded and dug in the spurs, getting a momentary added speed from her mount. Terry kept ahead of her and reached the town's main street a few moments later. One or two people were already hurrying along the boardwalks looking at the blaze. They swung round to watch Terry as he came galloping past.

"The four horsemen!" he yelled. "They did this— Put the fire out! I'm following the horsemen...," and then he was on his way with Hilda coming up at desperate speed behind him.

By the time he had gained the open trail beyond the town, Hilda had drawn level.

"This doesn't make sense to me," she said quickly, her eyes on the dim specks which denoted the speeding fire-raisers. "If Swainson or Burridge are behind it, why should they burn down their own places? The saloon and the Mayor's home?"

"Why not? They can always rebuild, and they will have moved all valuable stuff. *Their* aim is to get rid of everybody else: they can look after themselves.... It won't work, though. The alarm's been raised soon enough for the folk to put the fire out— Hello, they're turning off," Terry said abruptly, nodding ahead.

Starlight and moonrise, and the natural reflection from the sandy waste bordering the rough trail, made it possible to see the distant riders as they turned left, obviously heading back in the direction of the mountain range. Terry also swung left, murmuring in his horse's ear: "Keep it up, Smoky! Faster, fella! We've still a long ride ahead of us!"

The animal understood, but it could give little more speed. It remained more or less constant, which meant that the four horsemen were kept at their existing distance.

On and on across the pastureland, over arid stretches, through rocky areas, and so at last to the dim trail which led to Star Canyon. Terry kept on going, glancing once over his shoulder to see Hilda was not so very far behind. As the entrance to Star Canyon was reached, he slackened speed for a moment to give her the chance to draw level.

"Get your gun out, Hil," he instructed. "Just anything can happen around here."

She nodded in the dim light, her gaze fixed on the remote riders further along the stretch. Then she followed Terry as he went on again.

To gain the narrow neck of the canyon took perhaps five minutes, the horses' feet slipping on rubble and loose stones. Once it was reached, Terry looked ahead of him intently, having a full view of the canyon stretched before him. The stars were visible, reaching down at its V-shaped end. But against those stars were no signs of horsemen. Either they had moved at incredible speed to cover the remaining distance, or—

"Look!" Hilda said abruptly, and drew rein. Terry drew rein to find her pointing to the ground. The white dust carried the ploughed-up prints of a number of horses—which stopped suddenly and left undisturbed dust beyond. Terry stared at the unbelievable, and then above and around him.

"Same trick again!" he breathed, his voice harsh with exasperation. "There's got to be some explanation, and I'm going to look for it!"

He dropped from the saddle and hurried back on foot down the canyon until he came to the acclivity which led above. He was just upon the point of hurrying up it when a desperate scream from along the canyon halted him. Instantly he swung round, gun ready, and raced back through the dust. The scream was not repeated. He presently found himself back where he had left Hilda, but there was no sign of her. Only her horse, and his own, moving restlessly.

"Hil!" Terry yelled frantically, his voice echoing back at him. "Hil, where are you?"

There were no sounds whatever, except the soft moan of the wind at the mountain summits. Baffled, furious, Terry examined the dust. There were no signs of prints from the girl's high-heeled riding boots. No sign of anything, except two horses who could not speak.

For a second or two, Terry had a hard struggle not to believe in the supernatural; then he came back again to grim business and returned to the acclivity. Gaining the summit of it after a floundering ascent, he looked about him. Apparently nothing was changed from the daytime view. There were just the rocks, the distant view of the desert and pasture-land, not a thing moving. He shouted again and again until he was hoarse, without avail. Hilda had vanished as completely and enigmatically as the four horsemen themselves.

"Okay. This does it!" Terry snapped at last to himself. "I can't play this game with the gloves on any more."

In a towering rage, he returned to Smoky, mounted and trailed the girl's horse behind him. He reached Verdure again to find most of the townsfolk in the main street, the fires extinguished through the use of a human chain from the only water supply—a well-spring on the edge of the town.

Terry took a look over the assembly, then he stood in his stirrups and shouted.

"Hey, you folks! Listen to me!"

Immediately there was a stirring in the moonlight. Men and women, some of them in night clothes, came towards him. "My wife—formerly Miss Marchland—has been kidnapped," he said fiercely. "The four horsemen are responsible, just as they're responsible for trying to set fire to Verdure! The time's come to find 'em even if we have to tear down every rock in yonder mountains! None of you can doubt any more but what they're human, otherwise they couldn't fling lighted torches around."

"Nobody says they did," remarked Mayor Burridge, standing in his shirt-sleeves to the front of the crowd. "I guess phantoms have their own way of starting fires, Carlton."

Terry glared at him. "I *saw* 'em swing torches onto these roofs," he retorted. "You may be deceiving the populace, Mayor, by working amongst 'em here to quell the flames, but you're not deceiving me! I'll gamble Swainson's here, too, somewheres—"

"Sure thing," Swainson agreed, coming forward, his face blackened with smoke. "This fire had to be put down!"

"Why? You wanted the whole durned town burned out, didn't you? So as to get rid of the folks around here?"

"You think I'd be loco enough to have my own property burned out?" Swainson snapped.

"Yeah—for the bigger gain of emptying this whole territory! Stop playing games, Swainson! I'm not pulling my punches any longer! You and Burridge are behind this phantom business an' it's time the people knew it."

There was murmuring amongst the people. Swainson came nearer to Terry, wiping his face on his shirt-sleeve. Then with a lightning action he drew his gun. It was so rapid Terry had no time to counter it.

"Shoot your face off any more around here, Carlton, and I'll drill you," he said very quietly and deliberately, standing so near that the people around could not see his gun or hear his words. "Y'say you're not pulling your punches anymore? Okay, that suits me fine. I'll come into the open, too. Get off that horse and go into the Coyote there: I've got something to say." Terry hesitated, wondering if it was worth making a grab at his gun. Then he decided otherwise: Swainson would hardly be an amateur with his hardware.

"Okay—into the saloon," Swainson murmured, as Terry dropped to the dust. "Make it quick! And don't raise your hands and give it away that I'm covering you."

Terry moved, and found the gun of Burridge added to Swainson's. To the people Swainson called briefly:

"Hang around, folks. The Sheriff, the Mayor, and me have things to discuss. I guess we've some sort of a plan to hammer out after this attack tonight. Don't worry about what the Sheriff said. Maybe we're all a bit excited tonight." He laughed.

Terry walked into the still oil-lighted saloon, through it—under Swainson's directions—and into the private office at the rear. Swainson closed the door sharply after Burridge had entered, and Terry obeyed the order to turn around.

"Now," Swainson said, his face taut. "The time's come to put things on a proper footing, Carlton—and there ain't much beefin' you can do either if you want your wife back. I guess you made one mighty big mistake when you married Hilda Marchland: it makes her especially valuable to you."

"Cut out the preliminaries and start talking," Terry snapped. "What the hell do you want of me?"

"Stated simply, Carlton, you're going to get out—and stop out! And you're going to say as much to those people outside.... You became Sheriff because, to satisfy them, there was no other way out of it. But ever since you got into this territory you've been crampin' my style and that of Mayor Burridge. You know too damned much!"

"I've made it my business to find out all I can," Terry retorted. "You know as well as I do that you and Burridge are playing a crooked game—just as Marchland and Harrison were until they got rubbed out."

Swainson laughed unpleasantly. "Never mind what sort of game *we're* playing, Carlton. We got here first. We've tolerated you long enough, and since every other trick we've pulled has failed to drive you out, we're trying something new.... You won't ever see your wife again unless you leave town and go right back to where you came from. I don't just know where that was but, for the sake of convenience, we'll say Denver, huh? Far enough away."

Terry remained silent and Swainson's grin broadened. "Harrison didn't like you from the first moment he met you—and said as much to me. He got the idea from the way you were talking that you might be dangerous later on—and he sure wasn't kidding. You've been long enough in Verdure, Carlton—and the longer you stick, the tougher it gets for us to work out our own plans. So yore going—and before you do, you'll give us a good chance to get the people back on our side. Just like they usta be—scared outa their darned wits."

"Meaning?" Terry asked grimly,

"Meaning you're going to tell 'em that you think you've been wrong—that you believe it *was* phantoms who set fire to this town tonight. That being so, you've decided to quit the territory as yuh haven't the nerve to fight ghosts.... That'll make most of the population quit anyways. If you're leery, the rest of 'em sure will be. Then you'll get on your way to Denver and your wife will follow."

"You admit, then, that you are responsible for her disappearing tonight?" Terry demanded.

"Sure thing. You don't think I swallowed that line I got from you this morning about calling the whole thing off until you'd worked out a plan, do you? I didn't anyway. I had tabs kept on you, and, just as I thought, you and your wife sneaked off on your own for a look-see. After that you just naturally followed the horsemen—and lost your wife. I never thought such a nice chance would have come, like you wandering off on your own and leaving her."

"I don't see what you know about that," Terry said, puzzled. "After she'd disappeared, I rode straight in here to get help."

"No you didn't, fella. You looked around plenty. In that time I got the information of what had happened." Swainson relaxed and gave his hard smile. "Okay, so the phantoms are phoney," he said, shrugging. "But yore bangin' your head on a brick wall trying to prove it, Carlton. You never *will* prove it. It's the best gag that's ever been pulled in this territory—or any other. It'll clear every darned man and woman outa here finally and leave the pasture land free."

"For stolen cattle!"

"Could be.... Your wife guarantees you won't open your mouth too wide."

"Not altogether. If you send her to Denver after me, there's nothing to stop me informing Denver head-quarter concerning all I've discovered."

"'Cept one thing. You'll need proof. Authorities are keen on that. Can't act without it."

"I've all the proof I need."

"Yeah?" Swainson shook his head. "Not *all*, fella. You may have some invoices you stole from Burridge's home—a knife meant for your wife's back—the gun which killed Marchland—but you can't prove any stolen cattle, and you can't prove the four horsemen aren't ghosts, 'cos you don't know how they do their stuff. An' something else. Whatever proof you have up to now ain't goin' to help you any. You're gettin' out with exactly what you came in with—nothing."

Terry set his mouth. Swainson went on talking.

"Things like a knife and a gun are too big to carry about you, I guess, but you'll be searched before you leave anyway, and so will your horse's saddle-bag. Then you'll escorted right outa town. What proof you have will be at your home, I guess—the Marchland place. I daresay, bein' the honest, open guy you are, you've told your wife everythin' you've discovered. She'll tell us—so we can destroy it."

"If you touch her—" Terry clenched his fists.

"No 'if' about it, fella. We've our own necks to look after. All evidence must be destroyed. Try without evidence to convince the law officers in Denver, or anyplace else, and see what you'll get! Or mebbe you're not that crazy?"

"What guarantee have I that my wife will ever be released?" Terry snapped.

"None—but she will be, if she talks sense when we ask her questions. Y'see, fella," Swainson continued, "I'm working two sides at once. Gettin' rid of you and your wife, and at the same time using you both to convince the people around here that flight is the only safe course. *You'll* tell 'em so before you go; and your wife will tell the same story before *she* goes. That way the populace will be convinced. To shoot the pair of you will be easier, sure, but the people like you both, and it might be awkward answering questions—so this is the better way. Now how's about it? Ready to talk to 'em outside?"

Terry did not answer for a moment. He glanced down momentarily at his gun, weighing up chances. Swainson saw the movement and straightened his own gun up quickly.

"You'll forget that hardware of yours for the time bein', Carlton, if yore sensible," he warned. "I'd take it from you, only it might be noticeable to the folks and they'd wonder why you're not armed. Now get outside and talk, and if you flunk anything I'll kill you anyway and take my chance."

Terry moved forward and Swainson opened the door. He walked through the saloon with the gun to his back, Burridge bringing up the rear. By the time he had reached the boardwalk, Terry noticed that the people had closed in round the saloon in the moonlight and were evidently waiting' restively.

"Well, Sheriff, what about it?" somebody shouted. "Do we get a posse together and go chasin' these phantoms, or what?"

"Still sure they're human, Sheriff, with Swainson and Burridge back of 'em?"

Terry looked about him, then to the eaves overhanging the edge of the boardwalk where the saloon roof reached down to its gutter. He mentally measured the distance.

"I guess I got the idea wrong," he said deliberately. "The four horsemen are—"

He went no further. Abruptly his hands flew up, clamped on the edge of the low-hanging roof, and with a long vaulting swing he went hurtling over the rail and into the crowd below. Swainson cursed, his gun wavering. He couldn't risk firing in the poor light. To distinguish Terry amongst so many people was impossible. Then Terry's voice came constantly on the move, so he could not be pinpointed by the two men on the boardwalk.

"Folks, I take nothing back," Terry shouted. "These two guys here *are* responsible for the ghosts; they admitted it back there in their office. They figger to chase me outa town and kick the rest of you out, too. Right now I'm going to find my wife. If any of you want to help me, let's go—"

"What about these guys?" somebody yelled. "If that's the game they've got, ain't it time they was talked to, the hard way—"

Somebody fired from the edge of the crowd. Just in time Swainson jerked back, wood splintering from the roof pillar beside him. He fired savagely in retaliation…and that started it. A gun duel suddenly blazed out, the two men on the boardwalk backing into the safety of the saloon and sniping at intervals. For Terry it was a heaven-sent chance. He vaulted onto his horse, caught at the reins of Hilda's mare, and then beat it out of town as fast as he could go.

It was not long, however, before he realised horsemen were following him. Prepared for the worst, he slowed up, his gun ready, when out of the distance and moonlight, as the pursuers came into view round a bend in the trail, came a shout:

"Don't shoot, Carlton! We're friends!"

Terry was prepared to expect deception, then changed his mind as a group of townspeople, all men, came speeding up. There were perhaps a dozen of them.

"We're following along with you, Sheriff," explained the man who had shouted. "We're satisfied that you're on the level even if some of the others aren't. Wherever yore headed, we'll stick by you."

"We got provisions outa the general stores before followin'," another added eagerly.

"Nice going, and thanks a lot," Terry said gratefully. "How's about Swainson and Burridge? Have they been shot yet?"

"Nope. I guess we're the ones who did the shootin', then we figgered we'd better follow you. Those left behind are too leery of Swainson and Burridge to attack 'em, I guess. It's up to us to prove what kind of crooks those two are."

"I'm going to search for my wife," Terry said grimly. "When I've found her, I'm going to trace several thousand head of stolen cattle and try and solve the mystery of Star Canyon. I hope all of you know what it means, throwing in your lot with me?"

"Sure thing."

"We ain't worried, Sheriff. We always did figger Swainson an' the Mayor were crooked as rattlesnakes, only there weren't nothin' we could do 'bout it 'til you came along."

"It means," Terry said, "that you'll all be in the same class as outlaws. In fact, you won't be able to return to Verdure without risking a bullet."

"Them two critters running Verdure is the outlaws," one of the men snapped. "And we'll blast them before we've finished. Meantime we've got provisions an' th' hills ter live in."

"Can't want much more, I reckon."

"Okay," Terry exclaimed, relieved. "In that case let's go. I've got to find my wife before anything else happens...."

CHAPTER SIX

At the entrance to Star Canyon, Terry drew rein and looked about him. His followers gathered around in a group, their horses moving restlessly.

"I guess there are enough of us to make a proper search," Terry said finally. "I'll go straight forward along the canyon; an' you three fellas come with me. The moonlight's bright enough for us to spot anythin' unusual. Three more of you go up the left-hand cliff face, and another three up the right. Search every rock and crack and gully. We'll meet down here when we've finished. Okay? Let's go, then."

The various horsemen, their guns at the ready, deployed in the various directions Terry had indicated. He himself dropped from his horse and, with the three men he had ordered to work with him, began a careful study of the canyon floor. The moon had risen high now, at the full, its brilliance painting everything in a harsh pattern of black and white. Prints in the dust were easily distinguishable; so were the surrounding rocks and cliff faces.

Inch by inch, foot by foot, the ground was covered—until at length the narrowest neck of the canyon was gained. Terry came to a halt and pointed.

"That's the spot, fellas—see where those tracks vanish? Our job is to find why."

The men with him stared up at the cliff faces, their tops clear and grey against the shimmering stars. Dimly visible were the silhouettes of the other men investigating at the summit.

"I don't rightly see, Sheriff, how four horses and men could disappear right here," one of the men muttered. "Ain't even' reasonable. Can't turn aside and can't go up—'less they got wings."

"Fact remains, they vanished," Terry snapped. "And so did my wife, from right off her horse. She gave one scream—but by the time I'd gotten here she'd gone."

"Yeah? Sounds like this cliff face may swing aside somehow. Naturally balanced rocks ain't so unusual."

"I thought of that," Terry responded. "I can't find a trace anywhere. The cliff faces are solid."

There was silence for a moment, then a shout came floating from above.

"Any luck down there, Sheriff?"

"Not a thing," Terry called back. "How's it with you?"

"No dice. Ain't nothing but rocks and tableland. I guess it wouldn't be possible to lift four horses an' men up here with ropes, if that was how it was done."

"I suppose it wouldn't," Terry muttered, looking at the men around him. "All right, let's eliminate possible methods until we get around to the right one. They couldn't go upwards: it would be impossible to haul such weights without winches and cranes—and if Hilda had been dragged upward I'd have arrived to see it before she could have been hauled clear up the full distance.… And it isn't a moveable cliff: I proved that in daylight."

"So the only answer is the canyon floor—or ghosts," one of the men said.

"It isn't ghosts," Terry assured him. "Swainson's admitted that much. It's all very material and logical—so that brings us to this canyon floor. Okay, we all concentrate on that." He cupped his hands and yelled: "Okay, you fellas up there. Come down and lend a hand."

This done, he and the men with him strung themselves out in a line, which was soon augmented as the other men came from above. Then, over a dozen strong, they went carefully over the ground, so arranging their moves that not one section of ground was left uncovered.

So intent were they on their task that they failed to notice that half a dozen other men had ridden up and were at the entrance to the canyon. Swainson, grim-faced, watched the proceedings for a while, then he motioned his head and he, Mayor Burridge and the four gun-hawks accompanying them drew into the cover of the rocks.

"Just what I figgered would happen," Swainson said. "They're trying to solve how that horsemen trick is pulled—an' trying to find the girl, too, I s'pose."

"Let 'em go on trying," Burridge chuckled. "I guess

they'll not manage anythin' even if they stick around here for fifty years."

"Don't be too sure of that," Swainson retorted. "Carlton's got his wife to find, don't forget, an' he'll go the limit to do it. There's just a chance he might find out how the trick's done—'less we pull something first."

"Such as?" Burridge growled.

"Well, he ain't going out of the territory, as we told him, so mebbe we'd better take care of him after all and risk what happens afterwards."

"Shoot, y'mean?" one of the gunhawks growled. "Ain't so sure I like the idea uv that, boss. Must be more'n dozen men there—an' there ain't half that number uv us."

"Who's talkin' about shooting?" Swainson snapped. "I'm thinking they're right on the spot we want. Might be just one good chance to fix the lot of 'em at one sweep. Once we've gotten them in a bundle there ain't nothing to stop them vanishing for all time. Hop to it, Curly, and see what you can do."

"Y'mean—shove the rock?"

"Sure thing—and hurry up while they're all in one spot."

Curly nodded and sidled off into the moonlight. Swainson watched him go, and then turned as Mayor Burridge sighed:

"I don't like it, Swainson. Trying to nab all these men you may miss some of them. They'll escape, and in future they'll know the whole secret. I think you're taking too big a risk."

"Who is?" Swainson demanded, and in his sudden anger at being questioned, he forgot to keep his voice low. It travelled on the still air. Terry raised his head from his activities.

"Somebody there—canyon entrance," he muttered, fingering his gun. "Break up and move that way...."

The men around him nodded and began to drift away from their site of operations. Swainson, abandoning his argument with Burridge, peered round the rocks—then gave a start.

"Beat it!" he said quickly. "They're headed this way— Can't fight a dozen of 'em!"

"But Curly—!" Burridge gasped. "If he shifts the rock like you told him, it'll—"

"I'll grab him," Swainson snapped. "The rest of you get going back towards town. I'll catch you up."

He wheeled his horse round and jabbed in the spurs. To his annoyance, the animal whinnied in retaliation. Terry heard it distinctly and broke into a run, stumbling through the dust and loose stones, and watching intently for action as he ran.

By the time he had reached the canyon entrance there was no sign of any horseman. He came to a stop, trying to puzzle the thing out, the rest of his followers catching up with him.

"What gives?" one of them asked quickly.

"Dunno. There was somebody here: we heard 'em—"

"There's two!" one of the men snapped, pointing.

"Riding out there, heading for the trail."

Terry watched intently for a moment. Two riders had abruptly emerged from the cover of towering rocks some distance away, and were beating it as fast as they could travel. The moonlight picked them out distinctly.

"Damn—no horses!" Terry looked about him in exasperation; then the gun of the man beside him exploded. Not that it proved of any use. The two men went on riding, gradually becoming lost to view in the common grey of the pastureland.

"Be Swainson and his boys, I s'pose," the man next to Terry said, holstering his gun. "I thought I could pick one of 'em off and get him t' talk. Light too bad, I guess."

"Yeah." Terry's voice was thoughtful. "Wonder what they were doing back of those rocks there? It was something that delayed 'em or they'd have been on their way sooner. Might do worse than take a look. We haven't explored round the back there—only on the top. Come on."

He hurried forward until he gained the spot from which the two horsemen had emerged. At this point there were dozens of rock spires, large and small, jutting from the white dust of the ground. From the look of the prints in the dust two horses had stopped at this point, and quite distinctly one man's footmarks were visible leading towards a curiously-fashioned needle of rock standing in comparative isolation.

Terry, the men beside him moved over to it, following the footmark trail. It was a smooth-faced rock, almost glazed, and upon it, dimly visible in the silvery light, were odd symbols and traceries.

"Say," one of the men said abruptly, "that's bin part of an Indian shrine at some time. Them marks are Indian. Quite a lot of 'em scattered around this territory. Throw back to the Aztec days, I guess."

"We should have looked here sooner," Terry said quickly. a new note in his voice. "The old Aztecs were renowned for their mines, and shrines, and underground haunts. I guess Arizona is riddled with such places if y'know where to look. Just what did those two horsemen—or one of 'em, apparent from the prints—want with this?"

He moved a little closer, passing his finger-ends over half obliterated ancient Aztec signs. Then he frowned and pushed a little. It had seemed to him that the stone moved very slightly. There was no longer any doubt of it when he gave a vigorous shove. Naturally balanced by some long-forgotten Aztec engineering skill, the thin obelisk tilted until it was at an angle of perhaps fifty degrees from the ground.

"I'll be dog-goned!" one of the men exclaimed. "What d'you reckon that does, Sheriff?"

"It's a lever," Terry said, straightening up and considering the tilted stone. "What it operates I don't know. No sign of anything around here having changed position—but mebbe in the canyon—"

He swung round, everything else forgotten, and went back at a half run to the canyon, his men racing behind him. Halfway up it, where the walls narrowed, they slowed down. Instead of a continuous trail of white dust there was an oblong opening, like the entrance to an extremely large grave.

"We got it, fellas!" Terry cried excitedly, hurrying forward. "More luck than judgment, I guess, but this is it! Take a look...."

Breathing hard from their running the men stopped at the edge of the pit which had been born in the cavern floor. In its depths was total darkness, a wind blowing out of it which smelled of age and mildew.

"Simple enough," one of the men said quickly. "Swainson an' his boys musta found this ancient Aztec entrance to the underground an' the lever that works it. So they cashed in on the idea to manufacture four ghosts—I don't get even now how it works, but mebbe we will if we risk going below."

"We're going," Terry said decisively. "Or anyways, I am. I've still got my wife to find. Up to you fellas if you want to come."

He picked up a stone and dropped it into the hole to judge the distance below. It sounded as if it might be ten or fifteen feet drop.

"One or two of you stay above on guard," he instructed. "And keep watch on the horses."

The order given, he lowered himself over the rim, then dropped. It was a longer fall than he'd thought. He landed heavily with an impact which shook his teeth. Scrambling up he looked around him. He was in darkness on all sides, but the reflected star and moonlight through the opening above was sufficient to enable him to see he was on dusty ground—or so it seemed at first. It did not take him long to discover it was a solid oblong piece of stone, wide enough to comfortably accommodate four horses and men. Plainly, when the stone was in its normal place, it fitted exactly the hole above and drifting dust hid the hair-thin cracks where stone touched the natural cavern floor.

Right at this moment Terry had no time to admire the long-gone engineering genius which had produced this secret entrance to an underworld retreat: he was too concerned in thinking of Hilda's safety. He called a warning above, reminding his followers that it was a long drop. Then when five of them had dropped beside him, he began moving, striking a lucifer and peering into the dark.

"This ain't a tunnel, sheriff; it's one helluva cavern. Our voices even echo."

"I think you're right," Terry acknowledged. "Let's see how far we can get."

He found his way to the edge of the stone flooring, to discover it had come to rest about a foot from the normal level of the cavern. Jumping down, he struck another lucifer and held the flickering flame so he could see underneath the naturally hydraulic platform.

"Stone balances," he said, after a moment. "One diagonal stone bar on a massive stone hinge to the underside centre of this, platform. That connects with another long lever bar. All a matter of balance, I guess. Shifting that Aztec pole back in the rocks moves the lever bar and raises or lowers this platform. I guess that's logical enough. If you've a lever long enough you could balance the earth itself under fingertip control. Depends where you get your fulcrum. These guys sure knew their job—"

"Say, you hear something?" one of the men asked abruptly, as Terry's lucifer expired.

They were all silent in the total dark, hands on their guns. It was a darkness which aided their hearing, however, and presently they heard again the sound which had been apparent to the man near Terry.

"Cattle!" Terry whispered. "Lowing cattle—somewhere in this direction."

He began moving slowly in the darkness, the man nearest him holding onto his belt. The distant sound of cattle did not come any closer, though it still acted as a directive. Terry paused at length, feeling around him carefully—then he risked another lucifer. The momentary flame, flickering in a strong draught, revealed the opening to a tunnel.

"Down here," he murmured. "Let's go—and keep your hardware ready."

"Sure is some set-up," muttered the man hanging onto him. "With all this space below I reckon there ain't much Swainson *couldn't* do."

"There's space because we're going right into the mountains themselves," Terry responded. "So naturally we— A light!" he broke off tensely, pointing ahead.

From this distance along the tunnel it only looked like a yellow smudge, but as the men advanced towards it, it became brighter—until finally they discovered that the tunnel had ended in a cavern so vast it was overpowering. Oil lamps were fixed in the walls at, different points. The roof soared up into a dim, spiky mass of stalactites.

"Cattle! Hundreds uv steers," one of the men whispered. "I guess I never saw so many all in one place! Not that there ain't room for 'em...."

Terry was silent. Just at this moment he was absorbing the full height and depth of Swainson's grandiose scheme. Here in this vast natural space were numberless steers, corralled off by properly made fences into different sections. It was like viewing a mammoth ranch under a sky of rock, all of it dimly lit by the numerous lamps.

"Yeah, it's a smart set-up," one of the men said grimly, gazing down from the high rimrock of the tunnel's edge. "Simple too. Get the cattle, drive 'em across country to this canyon, then hide 'em. When finally they're released into the pastures of Verdure, the brands'll be gone so's nobody can identify 'em as stolen. Yuh've gotta hand it to Swainson. He knows what he's doin'."

"Dead right, fella," observed a cold voice. "Get your hands up—all of you. Quick!"

Terry did not need to look behind him to know he was dealing with Swainson. He found his gun taken from him, then with his hands raised he about-faced when ordered to do so.

"Sorry, gents, this is the end of the line for you,"

Swainson snapped. "I guess you all know too much now to be let loose with your information. For your benefit, Carlton, I might as well tell you that those men you left on guard are dead—and buried. Can't take risks now this hideout's been found."

"Where's my wife?" Terry demanded bitterly. "That's all I'm interested in right now."

"You'll see her," Swainson answered dryly. "I might even be generous an' let you die with her."

"This is a smart set-up you've got here, Swainson," one of the men said.

"Yeah. You wouldn't have found it, either, but for things gettin' a little outa hand. I figgered I hadn't enough men to deal with all of you when I followed you from Verdure. I was going to plunge the lot of you below here while you were searchin' the canyon floor, but you got wind of me. I had to call off the idea and beat it—then halfway back to Verdure it occurred to me that you, Carlton, might be smart enough to follow footprints and figger out the meanin' of that Aztec pillar. I came back quick and found you'd done just as I'd feared. Not that it matters now I've caught up with you. The stone's closed to the canyon, and I've a man on guard at the pillar. He won't shift it again until he gets my signal."

"What signal?" Terry asked curtly. "I don't see how you can give him one from down here."

"I can—and I shall, when I'm ready." Swainson grinned widely. "You don't think I haven't gotten this whole thing doped out properly, do you?"

Terry said nothing. He began to move as Swainson jerked his gun. Behind him, Burridge and the gun-hawks stood ready.

"There's a rough declivity to the left there, Carlton," Swainson said. "Get down it and keep going. Rest of you the same! Hurry it up!"

The command was obeyed, Terry going first down the rocky slope which led to the floor of the cavern. As he walked, his hands still raised, he studied again the extensive underground corrals and also noticed, stacked high against one mighty wall, the vast amount of fodder which had been stored. Just the same, this was no place for cattle. They needed the open air and limitless pastures if they were to survive.

To walk across the cavern took nearly seven minutes; then still under direction Terry and his men continued down an opposite tunnel of much narrower dimensions than any so far—and so into a smaller cavern.

Immediately a party of men got on their feet, guns ready—to lower them as Swainson and Burridge came into view. Terry stopped, relief sweeping him as he saw Hilda, apparently unharmed, seated in a corner on an upturned crate.

"Okay," Swainson said dryly. "If you two newly-weds want to start necking, get on with it. It's all you'll ever do, so you might as well."

Terry gave him a glance of contempt and then went over to where Hilda sat. He put an arm about her shoulders. "All okay?" he murmured.

"Uh-huh. They haven't done anything to me. I've just

been sitting here waiting for something to happen—I suppose you saw me disappearing and found out how the trick was done?"

Terry shook his head. "No. I heard you scream, but when I'd landed back where I'd left you you'd gone, there was just the two horses, nothing more. I had a lot to figger out after that...," and he went into detail.

"You'd hardly gone," Hilda said, "when the canyon floor began to lower. Two men came out, snatched me from my horse and dragged me below. Then they sent that platform up again—or somebody did."

"My men down here had instructions to capture any followers," Swainson said, he having drifted into earshot of the couple. "There are rock peepholes by which the canyon can be viewed. I've just been questioning them about your capture, Mrs. Carlton. It seems you and your husband here were seen, and the intention was to get both of you, but by the time the canyon floor had been lowered you, Mrs. Carlton, were alone—not that it matters. I have both of you now."

"To kill us, I suppose?" Hilda asked bitterly.

"Not because I have any personal grudge," Swainson answered, shrugging, "but because so intricate and far-reaching a scheme as this cannot be allowed to be upset."

"Can that platform only be operated from outside— at the Aztec pillar?" Terry asked, thinking.

"Does it matter?"

"Definitely. How can you lower that platform at a moment's notice if there's no man at work on the lever end? Such as when you captured my wife, for instance?"

Swainson hesitated. "It can be operated from outside or in," he replied. "All depending—as far as inside is concerned—if you know where to look. Naturally I shall not tell you the spot, just in case anything goes wrong and you have a chance of escaping. Normally, when the four horsemen are abroad, one man is on duty at the Aztec pillar. It is his job to open and shut the canyon floor for the horsemen to enter. He does not belong down here but is a citizen of Verdure— returning there whenever his job is finished for the night. There is a hideout near the pillar if anyone gets too inquisitive."

"Who is this citizen of Verdure?" Terry demanded.

"It doesn't matter, Carlton. Nothing does, far as you're concerned. You and your wife—and the men you have with you—are going to vanish from the map before tonight's out, and I'll gamble that all the authorities and lawmen in the States won't ever find out what happened to you."

"I seem to remember you gambling that *I* wouldn't find out about this set-up," Terry reminded him, and it brought a change of expression to Swainson's thin face.

"You turned out smarter than I'd figured," he shrugged. "Anyway, before I send the lot of you for the last drop—and I *mean* drop, down a mine-shaft located near this cavern—I want some information. Where have you put your evidence, Carlton? The stuff you've gathered up to now?"

"What use would it be my telling you if I'm dead and can't use it?"

"I still want to know. I'm not overlooking the fact that a man—or men—might come down here to look around one of these days—and if that happened any evidence you've planted might be found by this guy. It isn't worth it to me to take the chance. So where is it? At home?"

"Surprises me you haven't looked there," Terry answered dryly.

"I haven't had the time yet. You can save me a lot of trouble by talking. So where is it?"

Terry shook his head. "No dice, Swainson. Since you're planning on blotting me out anyway, I don't see why you should have that information as well. It's where it *will* be found if you dispose of me. I've seen to that."

Swainson was silent. Terry waited for the next. That he had lied had purely been to try and gain time.

"Okay," Swainson said finally. "Since you're stubborn, Carlton, mebbe your wife can be made to talk—if she knows anything. If she doesn't, then mebbe you'll open your trap to save her."

He signalled Curly, who came forward. Terry tightened his hands on Hilda's shoulders as he felt her tremble a little—then before he could say or attempt anything, he was seized roughly by the other men and dragged away. He made a savage effort to tear free, but it was no use.

"Before we start," Swainson said, as Curly drew up his sleeves on his massive arms, "you have one more chance, Carlton. Where have you put the evidence you've collected?"

"Don't tell him, Terry!" Hilda insisted. "I can take whatever is coming to me. I—"

"It's not worth it, Hil," Terry broke in quietly. "You win, Swainson. It's all in the safe back home. The Marchland place."

"Before I believe you, I'll make sure," Swainson said. "Is it a key or combination safe?"

"Key."

"Okay, let's have it. Curly can go back and investigate. I'll keep you two on ice until I know whether you've been lying or not."

Terry lowered his hand to fish for the key in his pants' pocket, but Swainson jerked his gun.

"No, you don't, Carlton. I'll get it."

He stepped forward. Terry remained passive as Swainson's free hand went into his pants' pocket—then he acted. He raised his right foot and slammed it down heel-first on Swainson's toes. He gasped; then he rocked as a fist whizzed up and battered under his jaw. One hand being locked in Terry's closely fitting pocket, he couldn't balance himself properly, which was just as Terry had calculated. Immediately he shot out his arm and held Swainson firmly round the waist, using him as a shield.

His gun gone, Swainson tore his hand free of the imprisoning pocket and breathed hard.

"Bad move that, Swainson," Terry told him dryly. "Right now you're my insurance for continued good health. Tell your men to toss their hardware over here, unless you want a bullet in you."

The men gathered in a circle, Burridge amongst them, hesitated. Swainson motioned urgently.

"You heard what he said, didn't you?" he demanded. "Get on with it!"

Again the hesitation. It looked as though each man was wondering whether Swainson was worth saving anyway—then, as he yelled the order at them furiously they obeyed, perhaps from fear of what might happen to them later if he escaped.

"Okay, boys," Terry said, still gripping Swainson mercilessly and glancing towards his own colleagues. "Use those guns—two to each of you. You as well, Hil."

His direction was obeyed. Only then was Swainson released. Terry took the two guns Hilda picked up for him and looked at the scowling saloon owner with a grim smile.

"Didn't quite work out, Swainson, did it?" he enquired. "And since I'm down here and got the upper hand for the moment, I'll add a few more facts to my catalogue of crime.... You wanted information from me: now I want some from you. Who amongst this bunch of beauties are the four horsemen, and how do they do it?"

"Do what?" Swainson snarled. "Damnit, you've seen how that platform works. What the hell more do you want?"

"They are white, and so are the horses. How is *that* done?"

"White suits and hats, special white coverings for the horses," Burridge replied, and Swainson glared at him.

"Don't waste any time telling him, do you?" he snapped.

"Safest. He's got the gun."

"I want those coverings," Terry said. "Be useful for my accumulating pile of evidence."

Swainson set his jaw and motioned one of his men. Evidently the gunhawk understood, for he went to a further wall of the cavern and from a natural alcove took out a pile of white painted coverings and white stetsons and riding suits.

"You boys take charge of those," Terry said, glancing at his own men. "Now for a few more points, Swainson, May as well have everything clear while we're about it.... Where exactly have all the stolen cattle come from, and how did you do it?"

Swainson was obviously not parting with any more information—but Burridge wasn't so tough. He began talking, despite the vicious look he got from the saloon owner.

"The cattle are all from ranches within a hundred-mile radius of Verdure. We operated with a gang of men we knew we could trust. They did the job at night, driving the cattle in the dark hours to Star Canyon here; then we brought 'em below. Because pastures are needed, we aim to empty Verdure of people."

"You mean you *did*," Terry told him grimly. "I guess that's no more than a pipe-dream now, fella. Thanks for the information, Mayor, which is more or less as I'd figured out. An' what about Marchland? He was a go-between, wasn't he?"

"Uh-huh," Burridge acknowledged. "He acted between us and the party who figure on buying the herds later."

"What party?"

"The name's Dixon. Over the border—New Mexico way. I guess he's a guy who—"

"Shut up!" Swainson blazed. "You've said enough already, Burridge! If I ever get outa this spot, I'll settle with you for this!"

"You won't get out of it, Swainson," Terry assured him, "so get that through your skull right now.... Dixon, eh? New Mexico? I never heard of him, but I guess he can be traced. I suppose you intended burning out the brands on these steers?"

Burridge nodded, but Swainson remained with his jaw set, his eyes, darting about the cavern as though he were trying to think out a method of escape.

"We're doing very nicely for details," Terry said, after a moment, "and all these men here with me are useful witnesses. Now let's get to something more personal. About Harrison. He shot Marchland, didn't he?"

"How should I know?" Swainson asked sourly.

"You should know, because you're the brains behind

everything, I don't think Harrison would have pulled a job like that on his own account. You told him to, didn't you?"

"You can go to hell, Carlton," Swainson replied.

"And Harrison himself.... My guess is *you* shot him. Or else you, Burridge...."

"It wasn't me," the Mayor said quickly, as Terry's eyes pinned his. "I swear it wasn't."

"I believe you," Terry said in contempt. "You're too damned yellow for me to do anything else. That brings it back to you, Swainson. What about it?"

"What kind of a mug do you take me for? Even if I did murder Harrison, you wouldn't expect me to admit it, would you?"

"You might—since you're cornered. Skip it for the moment: I daresay the law will knock the truth outa you in time." Terry looked about him, then added: "Well, that seems to be all we can do right here. Can't be far off dawn and we all need rest. We can grab it now and use guards in relays. Then you're going to start moving, Swainson—Burridge and the rest of you. Not to any phoney trial in Verdure, but to the best jail in the nearest city. Meantime, take it easy."

Terry turned aside, delegated several men to the first shift of sentry duty, and then relaxed on the floor with his back to the cavern wall. Swainson and his men were herded over to a corner, ordered to sit down, and kept under the surveillance of the four men with guns.

"I don't know how you can have the detachment to rest, and even sleep," Hilda murmured, sprawled beside Terry as he rolled himself a cigarette. "Suppose one of these men pull something?"

"They won't. Those boys who are on guard are solidly behind me. Nothing to worry over, Hil. Soon as I've had this cigarette I'm going to sleep. And you should do the same."

"Well—I can try, but I don't expect to be successful." But in this she was wrong. The exertions and nerve-strain she had experienced had a definite reaction now she felt comparatively safe. She began to doze as she watched Terry's cigarette lazily. For his own part he sat surveying the cavern, the men under guard, and then the pile of 'ghost' coverings nearby. He, too, felt the need for sleep creeping up on him, so rather than fight it he threw, away his cigarette and relaxed against the wall.

Swainson, forcing himself to remain alert, watched the half-consumed, still-glowing cigarette come to rest on the stone floor a couple of yards away. He affected not to notice it, relaxed, and pillowed his head on his arm with the apparent intention of going to sleep.

For a long time he lay watching the guards through his eyelashes. They kept their attention on him until they seemed satisfied he had dozed off. To give the right impression, he stirred restlessly and turned, flinging out his right hand from beneath him. It fell so that it covered the smouldering cigarette end, hidden now by the bulk of his body.

His back to the guards as he lay in apparent slumber Swainson worked fast. He breathed gently on the cigarette end until it was glowing brightly. Laying it on the floor close by his face, so he could breathe on it and give it life, he gently moved a cartridge from the belt about his waist, an action so stealthily done it merely looked from the back view as though he was stirring in uneasy slumber.

Still with hardly any apparent movement, he broke the cartridge in two and carefully plugged the open end with the glowing cigarette, the dead end being pressed flat on the gunpowder and the lighted end free. Inevitably, when the tobacco burned low enough, the gunpowder would explode, and before long.

Swainson stirred again and sat up. At the same moment as he had expected, the guards swung their attention on him, but in the split second before this happened he had rolled the cartridge some distance away across the floor. He saw it come to rest against a further wall, carried that far by the natural slant of the stone. He breathed in relief as he saw it still glowing. He had had to risk it that the lighted end would survive destruction.

"No damn chance to rest in this place," he said bitterly looking at Burridge; then without looking at him directly and covering his mouth with his hand, he added: "Be ready for action when you hear a gunshot. It's our last throw."

"Where from?" Burridge muttered, bewildered.

"Stop asking stupid questions. Just be on the alert."

"Listen, you—" One of the guards came forward. "If you've any talking to do, Swainson, do it out loud.

Whispering ain't allowed, see?"

"No, I don't see!" Swainson snapped, deliberately drawing attention from everywhere save himself. "You don't represent the law, and if I want to whisper I'll go right on doing it!"

"Yeah? Better watch yuhself, Swainson. It don't say because the sheriff hasn't beaten yuh up yet that *I* shan't. I'm takin' no back answers from a cheap crook like you—"

Abruptly the cartridge by the wall exploded. It had the identical sound of a gunshot. The guards spun round, startled. Swainson leapt up and landed a terrific blow under the jaw of the nearest man; then he snatched his guns. Without taking any pause he fired relentlessly, one gun after the other. Each guard went down, his hardware dropping.

Then there was a deadly silence. Swainson, breathing hard, looked around him amidst the cordite fumes. Burridge, astounded by the suddenness of everything, was still against the wall, blinking. Terry and Hilda, awakened by the commotion, were looking fixedly at the pointing guns. Around them the men who had gone 'off duty' were stirring into wakefulness.

CHAPTER SEVEN

"What happened, boss?" one of Swainson's gun-hawks asked, picking up the guns the dead guards had dropped. "Where'd that gunshot come from?"

"Never mind. I used my brains—which is more'n any of you jelly-kneed critters ever did.… You, Carlton, get on your feet. And your wife and the rest of the bone-heads with you."

Terry obeyed and helped Hilda up. At a signal from Swainson, all guns were removed from the group by the wall.

"Just as well I didn't talk too much, Carlton," Swainson said. "I had the idea I might beat you to it. Guess it's time you and those with you were taught a lesson. I'm carrying out my original plan to ditch the lot of you where nobody can ever trace your remains. Curly—tie 'em up. Separately. I don't trust 'em in a bunch—an' make a good job of it."

"Sure thing." Curly moved away and signalled two of the boys to help him. By the time they had finished their activities, Terry, Hilda, and the few men remaining in their party were so tightly trussed they could barely move.

Swainson looked them over, grinned, then glanced back at the sprawling bodies of the guards he had killed.

"Guess they got off better than you will," he said. "You're going down the mine-shaft. Those of you that survive the drop will be broken up just the same, an' the ropes'll make sure you don't have a chance to get away. Chances are the fall will kill you. I guess it's a good hundred and fifty feet down. Dry earth at the bottom. No soft mud or water to break your fall. I'll guarantee it makes the lot of you vanish from the eyes of men for good...."

Swainson stopped talking and signalled. His gunhawks came forward and between them hauled up the captives and bore them from the cavern and down a long tunnel leading from it. After perhaps a quarter of a mile's trip through dimly-lit passages they came to a halt at what was obviously an ancient mine shaft. The remains of a crumbling winch and cage were still there.

"Before I have you thrown down," Swainson said, "I'm willing to tell you something you're itching to know, Carlton—and I'm telling you now 'cos it can't do you any good. Poetic, huh?"

"Quite a sense of humour," Terry agreed coldly.

"I shot Harrison." Swainson gave a shrug and grinned. "I've got a policy, Carlton: if I don't trust somebody, or don't like him, I finish him. I've discovered it's the only way to get results. Like you, Burridge—shootin' your face off."

Burridge gave a quick, frightened glance. It seemed that his tubby little figure quivered.

"I said I'd settle you," Swainson added. "I'm doing it—now."

He fired ruthlessly—three times. Burridge's paunchy little body jolted in anguish at each shot; then, unable to save himself, he tottered helplessly over the edge of the mine shaft and vanished. After a momentary interval, there came a faint thud from his body as it struck bottom.

"You're getting trigger-happy, Swainson," Terry told him, his eyes glinting. "That makes about five in a row you've wiped out."

"Yeah—just as I told you. I obliterate opposition." It was plain that egotism and blood-lust were inflaming Swainson to the exclusion of all sanity. "Anyway, I was telling you—something you've bin wanting to know. I *did* kill Harrison. I was on my way to see him, and in passing the window I heard him about to say a helluva sight too much; so I plugged him and skipped outa sight. Nobody was near at the time. It was an easy job. Now ain't it a pity you can't use that information?"

"And Marchland?" Terry asked.

"I had Harrison take care of him. Harrison told me the way you were poking your nose in. I figured Marchland might talk too soon, or something—so I had him rubbed out. Wiping out Harrison afterwards was a good idea. It didn't only stop his big mouth about the phantom set-up: it stopped him saying that I'd given him orders to kill Marchland."

"Pretty wholesale, aren't you?" Terry snapped. "You also tried to kill my wife—or rather told Al Naycross to do it. Then when he flunked it, you shot him in the belly. I guess you've plenty coming to you, Swainson."

"Mebbe—but you ain't in any position to talk about it."

"What about that evidence you were going to check up on?" Hilda asked in sudden desperation, trying to gain time. "You said you'd make sure before you finished us, just in case we'd led you astray."

Swainson reflected. "Yeah, I did. I guess something might go wrong in that time, though. Now I've gotten you all sewn up, I'll gamble on it that you told me the truth. If you didn't, I'll turn Verdure inside out to find out where you hid that information. I don't see leaving it lyin' around: too dangerous."

He considered once again, then gave a nod to his men. Terry found himself seized. He couldn't struggle: he was too tightly bound. He was lifted from his feet, carried the short distance to the shaft edge, and then tossed into it.

"Terry—!" Hilda screamed in horror as he vanished; then she, too, was seized, lifted, and pushed over the shaft edge. She found herself falling headlong through darkness at a dizzying speed. During the fall she had no chance to think coherently: she was frozen with the expectation of death—

But it did not come. She certainly landed with violent impact; but it was not the bone-breaking force of hard ground. She had struck something yielding, and lay for a moment gasping, trying to collect her scattered wits. Then Terry's voice came from immediately below her.

"Fit to move, Hil?"

"Eh—? Yes, I— You mean I fell on *you*, Terry?"

"Right. And *I* fell on Burridge. Afraid the poor devil's done for, but he acted as a shock absorber with all that blubber of his. I dropped on top of him and he broke the force. In any case, the drop isn't anywhere near one hundred and fifty feet. I doubt if it's even thirty. Wriggle to one side," Terry broke in urgently. "More coming down. Let Burridge take the impact. I guess he's dead, anyway, taking the first fall to hard ground."

Bruised and aching, Hilda rolled herself to one side and heard the sound of Terry doing likewise. Lying on her back, still tightly bound, Hilda could see the dim yellow opening above; then it was blotted out as a bound body came hurtling down—to strike the 'cushion' which was the dead mayor.

In the space of perhaps five minutes everybody had been dealt with. Some five men, besides Terry and Hilda, lay sprawled in the shaft bottom, badly bruised and quivering with the reaction of expecting violent death. Terry began talking, inquiring as to how much damage had been done. Apparently there were dislocated shoulders, a broken arm, and severe shaking— but that seemed to be all.

"Bad enough; could have been worse," Terry muttered. "I guess Burridge proved useful in the finish, even if he was dead when it happened."

"Maybe death would have been better," Hilda said. "Trussed up like this, we can't do anything but rot, can we?"

"Anything but it, Hil. We have the advantage of being bound up separately. You and I are going to sit back to back, Hil, and try and untie each other's' ropes. Come on—no time to lose."

They began wriggling towards each other, making as little noise as possible in case it should travel to the top of the shaft. The men who had been injured stifled their groans as much as possible and just waited; meantime Terry and Hilda settled themselves firmly with their backs to each other, their finger nails digging into the tight knots, pulling—tugging—straining.

It was a long and difficult task with so little freedom of movement, but at length Hilda gave a murmur of delight as she felt her wrists fall apart under Terry's ministrations. She tugged sharply and her hands came free. After that it was only a matter of perhaps ten minutes to release every man.

"You guys who are damaged will have to put up with it for the moment," Terry whispered. "Sorry, but we can't patch you up in the dark. And tie these ropes round your waists: they may be useful later, knotted into one length. Right now our task is to get out of here."

"Back inter the cavern?" one of the men growled. "I reckon that won't do us any good, Sheriff."

"Not back there," Terry told him. "There must be some other way out. There's a draught down here which shows there is an opening somewhere around. If this is a true mine shaft, there ought to be a honeycomb of tunnels from the days when mining went on. I'll take a look."

He began to feel his way carefully about him, pausing when his outstretched hand came into contact with the rough wall. For a time he investigated it by touch, moving onwards in what he realised was a wide circle— Then, suddenly, emptiness. And a strong draught.

He began searching more thoroughly, still with his fingers. Though his lucifers had not been taken from him, he did not dare strike one in case somebody near the shaft top should see it. By touch alone, however, he was able to determine that the draught was blowing through a moderately wide tunnel opening. He returned immediately to where he could very faintly see the group standing.

"An opening," he murmured. "Don't know where it leads to, but we'll risk it. I've got a fair supply of lucifers: how about any of you boys?"

Apparently three of them were well supplied. "Good enough," Terry whispered. "Let's go—" Then he paused as one of the men objected.

"Look, Sheriff, d'you think that's such a good idea? We may only wander deeper inter the mine an' never find our way out again. How's about making an attempt to climb this shaft back into the cavern? Those guys above think they finished us: we'd have the advantage of surprise."

"Which, without guns, wouldn't do us much good," Terry said grimly. "I'm sure this is the better way. Wait a moment," he murmured tensely. "I hear Swainson talking up above."

They all became silent, as carried by the natural acoustics of the cavern the hard tones of the saloon owner came drifting down in snatches, apparently as he addressed his followers.

"...not worth trying simple methods any longer. With the...removed, probably dead, in the shaft...to clear out the rest of 'em from Verdure. They know... enemy. So we act...an' blast 'em out. Then...the cattle."

"What's he talking about?" Hilda whispered, straining. Terry did not reply immediately. He waited for the voice above to continue, but apparently Swainson had said all he intended. Instead there were sounds of movement.

"Near as I can gather," Terry responded, answering Hilda's question, "he thinks we're dead, or otherwise out of action, and is planning a full-blown attack on Verdure, the folks there knowing by now that he is an enemy. If he can clear them out, he'll then release the cattle to the pastures, following out his original plan."

"Which means that if we wait here long enough that cavern will soon be empty above, and we can climb up and get out," Hilda said.

Terry thought for a moment, then he said: "I can't see a guy like Swainson leaving no man on guard—just in case. Besides, if we wait that long, he'll be on his way by then. Our job is to try and get to Verdure ahead of him and warn the folks to be on guard. If we could only fix it in time, Swainson and his boys could run straight into an ambush which would finish 'em."

"That being so," one of the men said, "our only gamble is to risk that tunnel and see where it goes. Let's be movin'."

Terry led the way in the dense gloom to the spot where the tunnel opening lay. He stepped into the gap first, helped Hilda through and then the men for whom injury made movement difficult. Protected now by the surrounding walls and roof, Terry struck one of his precious lucifers. The draught made the dim flame dance, but he saw enough to realise that quite an extensive tunnel lay ahead, apparently with breaks in the floor which might precipitate them into further depths.

So, hanging on to each other, they began advancing— and it seemed to be an almost interminable journey. The tunnel turned corners, went up inclines, down slopes, and then straight for long periods, until it seemed it was never going to end. The only guarantee that it would lay in the draught constantly blowing along it from some point on the exterior.

"D'you suppose we're goin' round in circles?" one of the men questioned after a while. "Frum what I know of these kinda passages they just network in an' out uv the mountains and finish up where they started. Belonged once to the minin' galleries, I guess."

"We're not going in circles," Terry assured him. "All this time I get the impression we're not going into the mountains but away from them. And I don't think this is one of the mine galleries either." He paused, struck a lucifer and examined the narrow imprisoning walls.

"No," he repeated, when the flame died out. "Men never made this shaft: it's a natural blow-hole from some long-gone volcanic activity. As such it acts as a ventilator to the mine. What we are doing is following a natural air-shaft which might come up just anywhere."

It did, nearly an hour later, so Terry judged. The draught suddenly became much fresher, and ahead of them, at the top of a long enclosed incline, they could see a rough circle of stars. It gave all of them new hope and set them hurrying forward. In a matter of moments they had emerged into the fresh night wind amidst a tangle of weeds and a carpet of sleeping primrose.

"Some kind of gully," Hilda said, looking about her. "At any rate we're below the normal land level."

Terry nodded and hurried forward up the nearest grass bank. At the top of it he stood gazing about him. Perhaps two miles away reared the mountain range. The tunnel had evidently snaked that far from it. In the opposite direction, beyond an expanse of moonlit pasturelands, was the dim, hardly discernible huddle of buildings which denoted Verdure.

"Looks like we're two miles on our way to Verdure," Terry said finally, and in obvious delight. "This blow-hole through which we've come is only one of dozens scattered about this rough country. Best thing we can do is strike out for Verdure and see if we can get there ahead of Swainson and his boys—'less they've gone already."

"From the peace hanging over Verdure it doesn't look like it," Hilda remarked.

"That looks like the trail to Verdure, 'bout quarter of a mile distant," one of the men said, holding his injured shoulder tightly. "Swainson and his boys will come along it, I guess. How's about giving 'em something to delay 'em? A rope across the trail, f'r instance?"

"The idea's good but impractical," Terry responded. "We don't want to give him any clues as to what is coming. If he got tripped up, he'd guess we might be back of it and all surprise would be gone."

"Don't see why," the puncher argued. "It might be the folks of Verdure who fixed the rope. I guess Swainson's sold on the notion that we're out cold for keeps."

"We're not risking it," Terry decided flatly. "It would delay us too, an' we can't afford it. Let's be on our way."

Since he was in charge of the proceedings, nobody argued any further and the journey under the stars began. It was hard-going, exhausted as they all were, weary from lack of sleep, bruised and battered from their fall in the shaft; but they were motivated by the one thought that here was a chance to perhaps beat Swainson at his own game—to make him eat lead when he least expected it.

Apparently, though, the plan was not going to be so easy as that, for when the journey to Verdure had been half-completed, there came the sound of hoof-beats on the night air. The party stopped its advance and watched the trail. They said nothing and thought plenty at the sight of a fair-sized group of horsemen speeding along in the moonlight.

"Swainson and his merry men," Terry muttered. "No phantom stuff this time, either. Just a straight shootin' party, I guess. Too bad; I figgered we might beat them to it."

"What happens now, then?" Hilda asked, as the horsemen began to slowly disappear in the direction of Verdure. "Any use going on, or might we do more by returning to the canyon cavern?"

"We're going straight on to Verdure," Terry decided. "We still have the advantage of not being expected. We might be able to gum the works up for Swainson somehow."

So he went on doggedly, helping Hilda beside him, the men coming up in the rear. With no horses, and rough ground, it was a tough trip; and presently, evidently when Swainson his boys had reached the town, there came the sound of gunfire. Not long after it were flames, leaping from the town at the northern-most point.

"Looks like he's doing it properly," one of the men beside Terry said, striding on. "Last time he helped to quell fire, this time he helps to start it. Shows he knows how he rates with the folks in Verdure, anyway."

Terry nodded but did not speak. He was trying to think out some kind of strategy for when he reached the town; and by the time the trip was over, he'd more or less figured it out.

"Feel up to fighting a bit longer?" he demanded, looking at the weary faces in the reflected glare from the burning town.

"Sure thing," one of the men said, and the others, Hilda included, nodded stubbornly.

"Going to be tough without guns, though," one of them commented, and watched the confusion amidst the smoke of the High Street, where apparently a cross-fire of revolver shots was taking place.

"No reason why we should be without guns for long," Terry replied. "We've each got the lariats we were bound with. We can use them as strangle-nooses to drag down the horsemen that we know are the enemy. Altogether, we reckoned about a dozen or more men, including Swainson. What we want to do is capture the lot of them, if we can, and get them in a bunch—trussed and helpless. Once that's done, the battle's over. Only way to do that is to take advantage of the confusion and drag each man down where we can. We'll make the Black Coyote the dumping ground for them, and that's where we'll meet when we've finished, granting it isn't burned down by then. You'd better stick beside me, Hil; I guess roping gunmen isn't your job."

"I'm going to do my bit just the same," she said decisively, uncoiling the rope from about her waist. "Let's go before the job gets too difficult."

Terry nodded, motioned to his men, and with nooses in their hands they scattered, entering the smoke-filled main street and using the billowing black clouds as cover.

It became obvious to Terry and the girl as they neared the main centre of swirling horsemen that the fire was not so serious as they had imagined. As yet, only a couple of disused buildings on the edge of the town were alight—perhaps intended as a warning of worse to come if the people of Verdure did not give in—or get out. From the look of things, though, they had no intention of moving. They were sniping viciously from the windows of their homes, or round the doors of the general stores, the livery stable, and the stage halt. They were in every conceivable place which afforded shelter, spitting their lead into Swainson and his men as, using the smoke for cover, they fired relentlessly from the main street.

Dodging along the boardwalk at the point furthest from the fire, Terry glided along until he reached a position where a broad upright pillar afforded him good concealment. He held his rope already noosed, watching the swirling activity in front of him. How the rest of his men were going on he had no idea; up to now, there did not seem to be any diminution in the numbers in Swainson's gang.

Then one horseman came close by the boardwalk, intently aiming his gun at a lower window on the opposite side of the street. Terry's noose whirled out, settled dead over the man's head, and tightened around his neck. With a gasping cry, he was jerked out of his saddle as his horse shied, and came crashing into the dust. Instantly, Terry vaulted over the boardwalk rail, whipped up the man's fallen gun, then kicked the other one out of his left hand.

"Get up," Terry ordered, a gun in each of his hands. "Get on the boardwalk." The man gave a start as in the flickering glare he recognised Terry, but he had sense enough not to shout out his discovery to his comrades. Tugging the strangling noose from throat, he went up to the boardwalk, then came to a halt at Terry's command.

"Tie his hands behind him, Hil," he ordered, and she wasted no time obeying, using her own cord to do it.

Satisfied, Terry returned to the street, picked up the discarded rope the puncher had dropped, and re-noosed it. He waited, darting a glance now and again to the boardwalk to be sure the man he'd captured wasn't up to any funny business. Apparently he was not. He stood by the boardwalk rail, Hilda beside him.

Terry grinned as he saw two more horsemen suddenly jerked from their saddles by his comrades; then his grin vanished as, unexpectedly, Swainson himself came riding through the smoke. He had split seconds to get over his surprise at seeing Terry painted in the flames of the nearby building, then his gun jerked up to fire. Terry had the noose in one hand, and a gun in the other. He fired at random because there wasn't time to aim. The shot missed Swainson entirely and instead struck his horse. The animal reared in pain, sending Swainson's shot wide of the mark.

Before he could recover position, Terry's noose flashed through the air and landed neatly over Swainson's gun-wrist. A violent tug pitched him from the saddle of his already collapsing horse. He came down in the dirt and struggled up again, to find Terry standing over him, both his hands full.

"Call off this gun-fight, Swainson," Terry ordered. "If you don't, I'll kill you right now where you are. I'm not pulling my punches any longer."

"How in hell did you—" Swainson started to say blankly, then he jumped as a bullet spat dirt at his feet.

"Call it off!" Terry repeated fiercely, and he took the scowling Swainson's guns away from him.

Furious, and obviously baffled, Swainson got on his feet. He looked at the surging mob of men, then back to Terry.

"Fire in the air three times," he said sullenly. "That's the prearranged 'Cease Fire' signal."

Terry obliged, choosing a spell when the racket of crossfire had silenced for a moment. The effect was immediate. The gunmen in the street swung round, saw Swainson amidst the smoke, and did not immediately grasp the significance of the situation at seeing Terry beside him. They did when they found Terry's guns pointing at them. Nor was he alone. His own men, most of them armed by now, came following behind, ready for action.

In all, there were perhaps a dozen horsemen. Terry eyed them narrowly in the slowly dying glare of the nearby fire. "Set-up's the same as before," he said curtly. "One wrong move out of any of you guys, and Swainson gets it with both barrels. Boys, take their guns, then tell the rest of the folks to come out into the open and kill that fire for good before it spreads."

It took perhaps five minutes to follow out both orders. Swainson still remained standing, hands slightly raised, one wrist with the cord still dangling from it. Upon the boardwalk Hilda remained beside the man she had bound. The men on horseback, their guns gone, were pulled presently from their saddles by the people who came surging out from the boardwalks. There were men and women in all types of attire, most of them armed with guns or rifles, some even with knives.

"Looks like we've had a successful night in the finish, folks," Terry said, glancing about him. "Swainson figgered he'd got rid of me and my wife and the boys here, but he figgered wrong. And I'm naming him as a killer, fire-raiser, and cattle-thief. I've all the evidence I need and all the witnesses."

"String the guy up!" a woman yelled furiously. "He aimed ter set fire to Verdure t'night an' kill them as didn't leave."

"No stringing up," Terry answered quietly. "Not whilst I'm the sheriff. He and his boys are going to the nearest authorities for them to deal with him. I couldn't put him on trial here—none of you would be impartial as a jury—so it's up to outsiders, with all evidence laid before them. I've got that, and these boys of mine are witnesses to certain statements Swainson made earlier on."

There was a dissenting murmur, but nothing more. Terry, as the sheriff, had absolute authority in the matter of law.

"Tie this bunch up," he ordered, "and then cart them to the Black Coyote. We can stand guard over them there till we get some men over from Tucson to deal with 'em."

The people began stirring and moving, on their way to find rope with which to get the job done. Terry still remained where he was, his men beside him, pinpointing Swainson and his cohorts. Then, at a sudden cry of pain from Hilda, Terry could not help but glance in her direction. He saw her turning a somersault over the boardwalk rail, apparently from a smashing blow in the face. She crashed into the dust and remained still. At the same instant, the man she had been guarding was running for it down the boardwalk, his hands free.

Terry swung his gun round to fire, only to find himself knocked off his feet by the crashing fist of Swainson. For a second or two there was wild confusion, an exchange of shots, and then Terry found himself being helped up by one of his men.

"What the devil—?" Terry shook his head dazedly and fingered his gun.

"Okay, they didn't get away with it," the man beside him murmured. "Things just went haywire for a minnit—but the guy who slammed your wife around got clear, I guess. Not that one matters."

His confusion vanishing, Terry hurried over to where Hilda was lying. He raised her head and shoulders gently, then put his kerchief to the blood trickling from her split lower lip. She stirred in his grasp and opened her eyes.

"Bad, kid?" Terry murmured gently.

"If it is, it serves me right," she answered, struggling to an upright position. "Teach me to tie better knots next time. I evidently didn't tie up that gunman tightly enough. Suddenly I realised his hands were free, and he landed me a haymaker, and that was that."

Terry helped her on to her feet. "I'll be all right," said, holding a handkerchief to her mouth. "What else happened? Did the diversion give Swainson a chance?"

"Fortunately, no—thanks to the boys on our side. As to that mug who got away, he can be found later. An odd man doesn't make much difference, except that I owe him something!" Terry's eyes glittered dangerously.

Still with his arm about Hilda's shoulders, Terry returned to his waiting, watchful men, and the gathered Verdure citizens.

"Got 'em tied up yet?" he asked.

"Sure thing. Sheriff—all 'cept Swainson here. Didn't know if you wanted him hogtied or not."

"Just his hands. I don't trust 'em loose."

So Swainson found his wrists secured behind him. He stood smiling bitterly, until Terry swung him round abruptly and pointed to the dark bulk of the Black Coyote in the approaching dawn.

"Get walking, Swainson, to your own joint. And the rest of you follow him. In line!"

CHAPTER EIGHT

By the time Swainson, his men, Terry, Hilda, and the rest of the men and women had piled into the oil-lighted main bar-room of the Black Coyote, there was little room for movement—so much so that Terry looked about him in exasperation.

"What's the matter, folks?" he demanded. "Can't you trust me and my boys to look after these critters until we get the law officers to 'em?"

"Sure thing," a man said from the midst of the assembly, "but I still say we've more to do with it than any law officer. What in heck do they know about it in Tucson? Just because that's the nearest fair-sized place operatin' law and order, it don't say they should steal our prize."

"What prize?" Terry looked mystified.

"Swainson and these dirty owl-hooters who work with him. I say that the only fair trial there can be is by them who's been attacked—and that's us. In this room! An' everybody with me, I reckon."

"Sure thing!"

"You sed it, fella!"

And those who did not agree in actual words began

nodding their heads vehemently. Terry looked about him with a grim face.

"Look, folks, get this straight," he said deliberately. "You elected me as sheriff to administer the law properly, and that what's got to be done. All you want for Swainson and his boys is a necktie party, but I'm not permitting it. The crimes Swainson has committed— particularly in the case of cattle stealing—don't belong entirely to this territory; they cover the whole of Arizona and beyond it, so the next authority to deal with it is Tucson. I'm going to hand them the evidence I've got, and they can take it from there on. Now I want a volunteer to ride to Tucson and give 'em the facts."

There was silence for a moment, somehow menacing, then the man who had stayed at Terry's side most of the time gave a brisk nod.

"I'll do it, Sheriff. I guess I'm your unofficial deputy, so I can go to it—providin' I don't fall asleep on the way."

"Go at sun-up," Terry said. "That's in about another hour. Get some sleep until then, then be off. Meantime, I'll stay here with the rest of the folks and keep guard."

The man nodded and made to move through the assembly, but his way was barred. He tried once or twice and then gave it up, casting a grim look at Terry. He looked the people over steadily.

"Not giving me much help, are you?" he asked quietly.

"Ain't that, Sheriff. We appreciate what yuh've done, but we don't figger Swainson and his dirty rabble should go free. An' that's what they will do if the authorities get 'em. It only needs a shyster lawyer to fix things so's Swainson can walk out innocent. We *know* what he's done, the terror he's caused, the fires he's tried to start, the people he's killed. We're going to take him out to yonder sycamore at the end of the main street and hang him, same as they did afore all this bunk about justice took the sense outa livin'."

Terry looked at the man who had been speaking. He was a burly rancher, middle-aged, one who had obviously fought every inch of the way from babyhood.

"Can't allow, it, fella," Terry said. "I guess you—"

"Yore *gain'* to allow it," the rancher interrupted, his gun leaping into his hand. "Sorry, Sheriff, we've got our own ideas. Drop your guns. Bill, tie him up till we've finished with Swainson. An' get some rope on the girl an' those other men, too."

There was nothing Terry could do. He was forced to drop his hardware to the floor, and he stood passive but furious as ropes were passed about his wrists. In silence, he watched Hilda—her mouth cruelly bruised from the blow she had received—similarly treated. Then came the rest of his men. This done, the big rancher who had given the order gave a nod of satisfaction.

"No hard feelings, Sheriff," he said, shrugging. "Mebbe you just don't know the way we like things around here."

"It'll do you no good," Terry said bitterly. "If you hang Swainson without a properly constituted trial, you and those who give you help can be accused of murder."

The rancher grinned. "Sure, but I reckon you ain't the kind of guy to try and pin that on us, Sheriff, when we've rid the territory of a no-account rat. Okay," he added, snapping his fingers. "Bring him along and those other critters who've been working for him."

Swainson's expression changed. His thin face was sweating; there was plain terror in his dark eyes. He knew full well that at the hands of the vengeful townsfolk he stood no chance. With Terry there had always been the possibility that justice might have given him a loophole.

"Carlton, there's got to be some way!" he panted, as he was seized firmly. "I'm entitled to stand on my constitutional rights and—"

"Only thing you'll stand on, fella, 'll be buckboard— till it's driven from under yuh and there's a noose round your neck," the big rancher snapped. "Stop talkin' so much and get on the move. Go on—*git*!" and he aimed a savage kick that set Swainson walking forward uncertainly, held on either side by a powerful cowpuncher.

Standing bound, unable to move hand or foot, there was nothing Terry, Hilda, or the boys could do but watch. Gradually, Swainson and his men were manhandled out of the saloon, their cohorts being shoved along behind them, until at last the big room was empty, the dawn light creeping through the open door,

Outside in the main street, Swainson was bundled along unmercifully, shouting protests as he went. The real cowardice of the man was more than apparent now he believed his last moments had come. By the time he had reached the big sycamore tree at the end of the street, he was babbling promises, offering money, willing to sell every possession he had in return for his life.

"Yore wastin' your time, Swainson," the big rancher told him deliberately. "We've decided yuh'll hang, and that's all there is to it. So will these other guys along with yuh."

The gunmen who had stood beside Swainson in all his murderous deals said nothing. When it came to it, they had more rugged courage than the man who had directed them.

"Get a coupla buckboards from some place," the big rancher ordered, glancing at the men and women around him. "And some long lengths of rope. Haven't enough here to hang these critters."

Swainson gave up talking. He knew it was no use any more. He stood breathing hard, perspiration glistening on his face in the light of the rising sun. The outraged people of Verdure looked at him without mercy, then gradually first one and then another looked beyond him to the rolling pasturelands that stretched out towards the mountains.

There were sounds on the clear morning air—rumbling, distant sounds as yet, like an approaching thunderstorm or an avalanche in the mountains. Presently the rancher caught the noise, too, and he frowned as he gazed across the sunlit spaces.

"What in tarnation is that row?" he demanded. "Sounds like an earthquake someplace—

A woman cut him short. She was pointing urgently into the distance, the first rays of the sun sweeping across it and dispersing the haze and mist.

"Cattle!" she gasped. "Hundreds of steers. For land's sakes, *look* at 'em! Must be some kind uv a stampede."

Swainson turned to look as well. He did not know whether to feel relieved or more frightened than ever. From amidst the huge cloud of dust hovering over the pasturelands steers became plainly visible, travelling rapidly in the direction of Verdure, uncontrolled, in the midst of a mad rampage, enjoying nothing but the freedom of unconfined spaces.

"Those the steers you stole, Swainson?" the big rancher demanded.

"No idea," Swainson murmured. "Guess they must be; no other cattle around here in such numbers. Yeah, I get it!" he broke off suddenly. "That guy who escaped—the one who hit Mrs. Carlton. *He* musta done this. What for, I don't know."

"Seems plain enough," the rancher snapped. "When that guy made his break for liberty you were at the gun-point; he probably figgered that if he stampeded the cattle in this direction, it'd give you a chance to get free and smash down this town as well. It'll sure smash the town down, but it won't do *you* any good."

Two buckboards came rumbling up, pulled by willing men instead of horses. The big rancher turned quickly.

"No time fur a necktie party," he said briefly. "That stampede is headed this way, and I guess we can't turn it aside. We've got the sheriff, his wife, and those men to release. You boys hop to it and get it done. We've gotta move fast."

"And what about Swainson?" one of the men snapped. "We ain't goin' to let him get away with—"

"Nope. We won't hang him. Just tie him an' his bunch to this sycamore trunk and let the cattle do the rest. I guess it'll be good enough justice if the cattle he stole kill him off."

"You can't do that!" Swainson yelled as he was seized by savage hands and bundled back against the tree. "You can't—"

"Aw, shut up!" one of the men snarled, and delivered a hammer-blow which knocked Swainson against the bole. Then, before he could recover his balance, he found himself fastened securely, his men around him, the ropes being carried round and round, and finally knotted.

"That'll fix 'em," the rancher said, nodding. "Okay, let's be moving. Get all the horses you can, quickly."

Meantime, Terry had been advised of what was coming by the men who had released him, Hilda, and their supporters. The instant he was free Terry hurtled to the door of the saloon and looked out into the main street. The big rancher and his boys were just vaulting on to their horses, and a moment later came speeding down the main street.

"Ride like hell!" the big rancher shouted, as he came

past. "I guess this whole town'll collapse when that stampede gets here. There's horses at the back of the livery stable."

Then the rancher and his mounted colleagues were on their way. Behind them, without horses, came the men and women of the town, clutching a few of their more treasured possessions, some of them carrying children, all of them moving like leaves before a wind.

"What do we do, Terry?" Hilda asked urgently, staring at the distant dust-cloud and listening to the thunder of hundreds of hooves. "That rancher was right, you know—a stampede will bring this ramshackle dump down in splinters."

"You start running—to the north," Terry said curtly, and gave a glance at Hilda and the men behind her. "I'm going to cut Swainson and his men free."

"Don't be a durned fool!" one of the men objected. "He's a low-down killer, an' so are those with him. They deserve—"

"I'm a sheriff with a law to fulfil," Terry retorted. "Letting him die in a stampede, with no chance to defend himself, ain't legal, or even Christian. Now get going. I'm cutting him loose. I'll catch up with you later somewhere."

He vaulted over the boardwalk rail, dropped to the street, and began running. In a few minutes he had reached the spot where the demoralised Swainson and his men were fighting desperately to free themselves, watching at the same time the approaching herds, now no more than a mile from the town.

"What the heck's the idea?" Swainson demanded blankly, as Terry sawed quickly through the ropes with his knife. "You loco, Carlton? You've not that much love for me that you—"

"Shut up!" Terry snapped, as the ropes fell away. "Get on the move, all of you. Run like hell. I'll be right behind you. You're going to get justice, Swainson, but not this way."

With both his guns in his hands, Terry motioned them. Unable to credit that any man could have enough decency to free his enemy, Swainson just stared amazedly for a moment, then the growing din of the stampede set him on the run, his men beside him. They raced down the main street as hard as they could go, Terry hurrying up in the rear with his guns ready.

The boardwalks were deserted now. Everybody had moved, and was going on moving, to the north. Out there in the open space it would be possible to dodge the raging feet; right here in town it was asking for death.

Terry looked behind him as he ran. The first of the uncontrolled beasts was already nearing the sycamore tree. So much he had time to notice; then, just as he turned frontwards again to once more cover Swainson and his men, he saw Swainson throw something. So quickly did it happen Terry had no time to act before a large-sized stone struck him violently on the forehead. He tumbled over on his face, his head exploding, half the senses knocked out of him.

By the time the daze had gone out of his brain,

Swainson and his boys were out of sight. Terry staggered on to his feet, picking up his guns and holstering them; then he swung round at the sight of the first of the steers blundering wildly toward him. Immediately he dived to one side across the street, tumbling down the narrow space between one of the buildings. Just here stood the livery stable; a few horses were still pawing the earth restlessly and straining at their reins.

Given a few seconds respite before the full onslaught of the stampede crashed down on the town, Terry slashed through the reins of three of the horses and set them moving. The fourth and last he used for himself, leaping into the saddle and digging in on the spurs savagely.

With a whinny, the horse got moving, leaping out of the building, then swinging right down the narrow passageway between the buildings. With seconds to spare, Terry came out in the main street again, a solid, packed mass of crazy steers immediately behind him. He rode as never before, pursued by the din of hoofs and the rumbling crash of tearing timbers and collapsing wooden boardwalks and roofs.

He knew that in those few brief moments when he hurtled out of the town he was taking a gamble with death. If the horse stumbled, or he himself were somehow jolted from the saddle, nothing could save him going down under the murderous feet; but his luck held and he kept going, slowly widening the distance between himself and the nearmost line of cattle ploughing through the shattering town.

At last he flashed beyond the town and hit the trail, coming almost immediately upon the struggling people who were still on the move. One of the first people he saw was Hilda. He swung down from the saddle and hurried to her.

"Terry!" she gasped thankfully. "I was wond— What's happened to your forehead? It's bleeding—"

"Swainson," he retorted. "He threw a stone at me when I released him. I'll get him later. Right now, we've got to act fast. Get a fire going!" he ordered, swinging round on the people. "Right across the trail. It'll divert the cattle to one side. And for heaven's sake hurry up!"

The men in the assembly jumped to assist him as he dragged dry weeds and small bushes from the side of the trail and set fire to them hurriedly with a lucifer. Bush was piled on bush; the flames fanned by the stiff morning breeze, until a broad line of fire was right across the trail. The stampeding cattle —slowed up by the tangled debris of the town they had shattered— came into view at last, their numbers spaced out more than they had been, which made gaps in the solid wall of bone and sinew.

Tensely waiting with their guns behind the flames, Terry and the men of the party watched what happened next. But the strategy worked. Though the line of fire was not particularly dense, it was enough to scare the cattle. They shied when they came towards it, and careered off to left and right, blundering through the grass of the pastureland and there dispersing somewhat and slowing down from sheer exhaustion.

Just the same, Terry took no chances. He and the rest of the men kept the fire blazing furiously. It was as well they did, for dozens more cattle still came hurtling out of the shambles that had been Verdure; and, like the cattle before them, they swung aside when the flames barred their path. Then at last the onslaught began to cease. Terry looked about him and pointed to the dozens of steers scattered around the pastures. Their panic stampede was over. Docile once more, they were grazing at the rich grass.

"Okay, it's over," Terry said at length, looking about him. "And I guess Verdure's about in ruins, from what can be seen of it here."

The men and women were silent for a moment. Through the trees nearby could be seen the tangled mass of broken timber beams and fallen walls which had been the town.

"I guess Swainson achieved his object after all," one of the men said grimly. "He got the stolen cattle into the pasture and blasted us out of house an' home."

"And made good his escape!" It was the big rancher who spoke, as he came riding up from the rear of the crowd. "I hope yore satisfied, Sheriff! You released him and got a stone at your head fur your generosity. Some guys are suckers!"

"At least he gets no benefit from the cattle," Hilda said. "He has made himself into an outlaw."

"But not for long," Terry said, taking out his guns and examining them. "I've an account to settle with

Swainson. I'm going after him. The rest of you folks get back to Verdure and do what you can to rebuild the ruins. Some of you had better get these cattle straightened out, too. Fortunately, they've been released before the brands could be changed, so they can be returned to their owners."

Terry slipped the guns back in their holsters and turned to his horse. He paused as Hilda caught his arm.

"Since Swainson has made himself an outlaw, Terry, can't you leave it that way?" she pleaded. "He'll never dare to come back to Verdure. He'll just have to keep going on and on, with those men of his."

"I've got my job to do, Hil; I mean to finish it." Terry patted her arm gently. "You go back with the folks and try and salvage what you can of our home. And soon as you can, get some rest and attention for that mouth of yours. It's badly knocked about."

"I'll get over it." Hilda brushed the issue aside lightly. "It's *you* I'm worrying over, Terry. Chasing after Swainson is too much like committing suicide. Besides, you have no idea where he is."

"I'll pick his trail up. He can't have gone far, he had no horse, remember. None of us have moved beyond this point, so whatever footprints there are should belong to him and his boys." Terry kissed Hilda's cheek gently and then swung in the saddle. "That's the way it has to be, Hil. I'll be seeing you."

He nudged the horse forward and left the group. In a moment or two, he was alone on the trail, watching the white dust intently. There were no prints, however.

Evidently Swainson had been smart enough to think of that and had escaped through the grassland where no trail could show.

So Terry kept his attention first on one side of the dusty track and then on the other, but he failed to see anything beyond the pastures drenched in the sunlight. There was no sudden brief glimpse of men moving, no stray shots. Then it occurred to him there couldn't be any shooting, anyway. Swainson had gone without his gun, unless he had wrested one from somebody in his travels.

Half an hour later Terry was no nearer sighting his quarry. He drew to a halt on a rise in the trail and peered around him. To look for Swainson without a track was pretty much of a fool's game. He had only got to stay lying low to get away with it. Here in this limitless waste there could not be a greater advantage on his side.

As he sat and thought it out, ideas came to Terry. Swainson might hide indefinitely, but he couldn't do it without food. In Verdure he wouldn't stand a chance if he tried to get any, but at the mountain retreat there was all the food he needed. Sooner or later he would probably go there, or one of his men would. And having no horse, it would take a fair time to do it.

Terry nodded to himself, spurred his horse again, then headed for the mountains as fast as he could go. Before long, he reached the foothills, and from here went on to the nearby entrance of Star Canyon. Exactly as he had hoped—and expected—the hole in the canyon floor was open. He dismounted some distance from it, tied his horse to a shrub, then—remembering that he could be observed through peepholes in the rocks—he made a cautious advance forward.

Nothing happened. He reached the hole without getting a bullet in him. Taking a risk, he slid over the edge of the cavity and prepared to drop; then he changed his mind, as at the opposite end of it he saw a long wooden ramp was in position, a contrivance of rutted boards, up which the cattle presumably been driven before descending upon Verdure. He had wondered how the cattle had been stampeded from the underground cavern.

There was a quietness about everything which Terry found uncomfortable. It was hard to understand why everything was left open—too much like an invitation to walk to death. Nonetheless, he began moving cautiously down the slope the depths, both his guns ready, and still nothing happened.

When he reached the base of the shaft, he understood. There was a sight which made him wince a trifle. Caught in the massive balancing stones which operated the levitating platform was the gunman who had escaped from Hilda: knocking her out. Terry recognised him in the dim light. He was not dead, but one leg and arm were tightly imprisoned and blood was smearing the stonework.

"Fur heaven's sake," he whispered, half-conscious but aware somebody was there, "git me outa this."

"Do what I can," Terry assured him, and moved to

where the man was trapped. But it only took him a few moments to realise there was nothing he could do. The big top stone which controlled the stone bar operating the platform had slipped out of place, and obviously the gunman had not moved out of the way fast enough.

"Hurry up," the man whispered, his face wet with sweat. "I can't stand no more of this. Me arm an' leg are crushed

"There are two answers," Terry told him. "Either I cut you free, which amounts to amputation without any guarantee you won't die from loss of blood, or I put a bullet in you. You're fixed here, but good."

The trapped man groaned a little and closed his eyes. Terry waited, his guns ready.

"What happened, anyway?" he asked, after a moment.

"I—I shoved too hard on the balance rock." The man opened his eyes again. "That's how yuh—yuh operate the platform thing from inside. Guess it's jammed fur good now, with me in it. I'd let all the cattle free and wus going to close the hole when it happened. I've been stuck here since."

"What was the idea of freeing the cattle, anyway? I thought you were on the side of Swainson."

"I was till recently then he kicked me around for somethin' I sed which he didn't like. I figgered I'd get even first chance could. This was it—to turn his blasted cattle loose—an' mebbe wreck Verdure, too. The folks of Verdure were on the prod fur me, just as much as fur Swainson. I took care of the two guys who wus in the cavern back yonder on guard, then—then I did me stuff. I guess I didn't expect ter end up like this."

"Would you be the guy who's been in charge of the Aztec pillar outside?" Terry demanded. "The one who let the four horsemen in here after their night's work had been done?"

"Yeah, sure thing. Fur heaven's sake," the man broke off, with half a scream, "ain't there somethin' you can *do*—?"

"I guess so," Terry responded, and he fired once—straight to the heart. With a sobbing gasp, the trapped man relaxed, still held by his grisly arm and leg.

For several moments Terry was motionless. It had not been easy to kill the man, but it had been the only merciful course. Death would have come anyway before long—much more lingering. He turned and looked at the jammed stonework, then he moved over to the wooden ramp and examined it. It had been made of timber lengths, apparently, with struts hammered on to one side to give support to the feet of the cattle. At one end of it—the end which touched the canyon floor above—were quadruple ropes slung over the pulleys and operated by a hand-winch. To raise the ramp to the desired angle was therefore a simple matter. Evidently the cattle had been brought in by this method—just as they had been allowed to escape.

Then Terry's thoughts drifted back to Swainson. Sooner or later he ought to arrive, or somebody who could say, under persuasion, where he was hiding. So Terry withdrew into the shadow at the furthest extremity of the ramp and waited for something to happen. Evidently he would have things his own way down here, since the guards had already been rubbed out. He relaxed but remained attentive, his eyes on the opening above. Then, suddenly, an annoying thought occurred to him. He had left his horse a little further down the canyon. If Swainson saw that, as inevitably he would, he would be instantly prepared for trouble. The realisation of this was no sooner in Terry's mind than he was speeding up the ramp and back into the daylight.

A quick look around him revealed the canyon still empty. His horse was where he had left it, fastened to the bush some yards away. He headed towards it, but before he could reach it something whistled through the air above him and fell about his neck. Too late, he realised it was a noose. He was flung from his feet, his guns jerked from his hands. By the time he had torn the choking rope from his throat he was staring not only at Swainson, now with both the fallen guns in hands, but at his unarmed men behind him.

"I was just thinkin' I'd have to come after you, Carlton," Swainson commented grinning' in triumph. "I knew you were down there 'cos of your horse. Nice of you to come up and be so obliging. The rope was the one they fastened me and my boys to the sycamore with—the one you cut apart. I figgered we might use it later. I was right. Okay, you can come up. I don't aim to kill you just yet."

"Big of you," Terry growled. "What's the idea of

reprieve?"

"It's not a reprieve, Carlton. 1 mean to cash in on what's happened. The cattle are in the pastures, and Verdure's in ruins—just the way I wanted it. The only thing wrong is the people aren't away from the territory. So I guess it's to their big, good-natured hearts whether they want you to die, or whether they'll quit and let you live."

"Meaning I'm a bargaining factor?"

"Right. I release you unharmed if they get on the move."

"They don't love me that much, Swainson, and even if they did and you did release me, I'd hound you down the minute I was free. I'd never rest until you're either dead or brought to trial. That's straight."

"Mebbe." Swainson eyed him narrowly, then turned to one of his men. "Len, get back to Verdure and tell those mugs there what the set-up is. They can have Carlton back if they agree to get on their way by sundown. They might as well: Verdure's in ruins, anyways."

"Expect me to go back there and git lead in me belly?" Len demanded. "I ain't loco, boss."

"You'll get lead right now, you louse, if you don't do as 1 tell you. They won't shoot you until they've heard what you say. They're kinda righteous that way. Now start movin'."

Len gave an uneasy look, turned to Terry's horse, mounted it, then began the ride back over the pastures to Verdure. Swainson motioned with the guns.

"We'll go below, Carlton," he said. "There's grub down there, an' it's outa this blasted sunlight. After you."

Terry began moving, keeping his hands raised. He gained the ramp and went slowly down it, Swainson and his three remaining men coming along in the rear. Then when Swainson saw the imprisoned corpse in the stone gears, he stopped and stared fixedly. It was a wrong move to make, too. Terry took instant advantage of the distraction and twirled round, lunging out with his fist.

Swainson jerked his head to one side just in time and fired, but he was some seconds late, and the force of Terry's body cannoning into him deflected his aim. The bullet snicked stone somewhere, then Swainson really went down for the count as Terry spun about and came up with his left. The dim light stopped Swainson timing when to dodge and he got the fist clean in one eye. He toppled backwards on the slope, caught his foot in one of the wood slats, then crashed over.

Terry dived for him, twisting out of the grip of the three other men who hurtled on top of him. He fell flat on the gasping Swainson, missed getting the guns, but nonetheless kicked out of reach in the shadows.

Then hell descended on Terry as the three gunmen clawed, kicked, and battered at him, Swainson undermost and gasping with anguish as he, too, got the shock of the blows meant for Terry. Terry kicked out one foot and got in a lucky blow, doubling one man up with his hands at his stomach. The remaining two men redoubled their attack. Some of the blows Terry was forced to absorb, his head singing in consequence, but one savage punch missed him entirely and instead struck Swainson in the mouth. He gave a yell of pain and swore,

"Sorry, boss—" the man gulped; then his words snapped off as his jaws slammed together under the impact of Terry's right fist. The man jolted upright and lost his balance, his tongue guillotined at the end and bleeding furiously.

Terry used every trick he could, foul and otherwise. With so many enemies, he had no time to be ethical. He brought his knee up into the stomach of the remaining man, then with his hands Terry caught the man at the back of the neck, dragged him down, overbalanced him, then pitched him several feet away.

Up came Swainson's right, and Terry jolted back as he took it on the ear. He crashed down his right fist in retaliation, and it added anguishing fire to Swainson's already bruised mouth.

But the ascendancy for Terry could not last long. One of the gunmen picked up the weapons from the shadows, and levelled them. Breathing hard, aching and bleeding from onslaught, Terry rocked into an upright position and held up his arms. Swainson got up, too, a hand at his damaged mouth.

"Okay, Carlton, that settles it," he said bitterly. "I was going to hand you back in one piece in return for Verdure. After this, I've changed my mind. I'll get Verdure by my own methods and finish you right now! Give me those guns, you," he added, to the man holding them.

They changed hands. Terry remained motionless. He heard the hammers cock. Around him the gunmen were groaning a little from the punishment they had taken.

"This is it, fella," Swainson said grimly—then he broke off and twirled as one of his men gave a shout.

"Look out, boss—above yuh!"

Terry glanced up. On the rim of the cavity stood a small group of men and women, looking down. Hilda was amongst them, pointing into the depths. These facts registered in split seconds in his brain, as they did in Swainson's—then Swainson fired his guns. Above, three figures dropped, Hilda amongst them. Almost instantly a volley of shots came from above. The impact of the bullets swung Swainson round dizzily, clutching at his chest, across which a red stain appeared on his shirt. He half-tried to raise his guns again, then more bullets crashed into him. He dropped helplessly, the guns falling from him.

The remaining gunmen made to dive at them, but Terry was quicker. He tripped the nearest man up and stopped the next one with a vicious left jab. Then he had both the guns in his hands and jerked them fiercely.

"Up that ramp, all of you!" he barked out. "Quick, damn you!"

The men obeyed, hands raised. Terry took one moment to satisfy himself Swainson was riddled, then he hurried up the slope, left the gunmen to the care of his rescuers, and went straight over to Hilda. She was still conscious, but her hand was gripping her shoulder painfully. In a moment Terry had ripped the blouse sleeve away and examined the wound. He sighed with relief.

"Bullet passed on, kid," he murmured, making a pad out of his kerchief. "Just scored you, that's all."

"Worth it, to save you," she said, smiling faintly.

Terry looked about him at the gathered men and women, and then he frowned. Foremost amongst the rescuers was the big rancher who had attempted the necktie party. Terry realised now it had been he who had done the shooting which had got Swainson.

"What gives?" Terry demanded. "How come you all arrived at the right moment?"

"Y'can thank your wife fur that, Sheriff," the big man replied. "She insisted our job was to help *you* and let Verdure wait till afterwards, so we followed right after you. I guess you were in sight all the way to the foothills; figgered you wus making for Star Canyon. We'd nearly got to it when we saw a horseman riding towards us. He came out with some phoney spiel about us having you safe it fur Verdure, so I shot him dead."

"You what?" Terry asked, starting.

"Shot him." The rancher shrugged. "He was a no-account killer anyways. We'll never have peace in this territory till we blot out every black-hearted skunk that's in it. I shot him after he'd told us you an' Swainson were in the canyon here. I guess that's all there is to it. If you want ter try me for murder, I'm pleadin' self-defence."

Terry shrugged. "I'm not trying you for anything, old-timer, after the way you saved me down there. And I don't need to bring the law in, either. Swainson's paid for everything at one sweep, and these two remaining guys hounded outa the territory for keeps. As for the evidence I collected, I guess I can turn it in and explain that Swainson got what was coming to him."

"Or destroy it and start again," Hilda said. "That would be better, Terry. Return all the stolen cattle, rebuild Verdure, and make a fresh beginning."

"Up to the rest of you," Terry said, looking about him. "Mebbe you still don't want me as sheriff?"

"Yeah, we do," said the big rancher, grinning. "Only I still say you're too soft-hearted. Shoot to kill fust time."

"I'll remember." Terry raised Hilda gently to him. "That is, if I need to," he added. "From the way this territory's been cleaned out, I guess we might be able to live henceforth without ever drawing our guns."

With his arm around Hilda, Terry held her close to him; despite the pain of her shoulder she smiled up into his eyes. There was a strange silence about the folk of Verdure as they looked at the happy couple, then the big rancher grinned again as he yelled:

"Folks, as your self-appointed deputy sheriff, I call for three cheers for the sheriff and his missus!" The crowd laughed and shouted their approval.

Up the walls of the canyon the cheers echoed and re-echoed, heralding the beginning of a new and law-abiding life for the people of Verdure.

ABOUT THE AUTHORS

British writer JOHN RUSSELL FEARN was born near Manchester, England, in 1908. As a child he devoured the science fiction of Wells and Verne, and was a voracious reader of the Boys' Story Papers. He was also fascinated by the cinema, and first broke into print in 1931 with a series of articles in *Film Weekly*.

He then quickly sold his first novel, *The Intelligence Gigantic*, to the American magazine, *Amazing Stories*. Over the next fifteen years, writing under several pseudonyms, Fearn became one of the most prolific contributors to all of the leading US science fiction pulps, including such legendary publications as *Astounding Stories*, *Startling Stories*, *Thrilling Wonder Stories*, and *Weird Tales*.

During the late 1940s he diversified into writing novels for the UK market, and also created his famous superwoman character, The Golden Amazon, for the prestigious Canadian magazine, the Toronto *Star Weekly*. In the early 1950s in the UK, his fifty-two novels as "Vargo Statten" were bestsellers, most notably his novelization of the film, *Creature from the Black Lagoon*.

Apart from science fiction, he had equal success with westerns, romances, and detective fiction, writing an amazing total of 180 novels—most of them in a period of just ten years—before his early death in 1960. His work has been translated into nine languages, and continues to be reprinted and read worldwide.

Matthew W. Japp was born in Glasgow on January 16, 1914, and moved to Manchester at the age of nine, where he later won a scholarship to Manchester Central High School. As was the convention at that time, he left school at fourteen, and his family moved to Blackpool, where young Matthew became the breadwinner when he started working with a grocery firm (his father being unable to work because he had been gassed during the Great War). He worked so assiduously that he was promoted to Branch Manager, and pursued a highly successful career in the grocery trade until his retirement.

During the War he was a special operator in the Royal Corps of Signals and served with the 8th Army in the desert, Malta, Sicily, and Italy. He was posted back to England in time for D-Day, then battled through Normandy, Holland, and Germany, gaining a mention in dispatches. On his return to Blackpool on demobilisation, he met John Russell Fearn and the two men became firm friends.

Fearn had founded the Fylde Writing Society, of which he was Chairman, and Japp became a member, along with his Belgian-born wife Nini. At first Japp had aspirations to write a book based on his action-packed war memoirs, but Fearn persuaded him that there were better opportunities in writing popular fiction, so Japp shelved his war memoirs—a decision he very much came to regret in later years.

After the war, Fearn had diversified from being a specialist science fiction writer to embrace detective novels, westerns, and even romantic fiction, and he was regularly weighed down with commissions to write westerns for several publishers at the same time. Japp had a facility for plotting novels, but lacked the experience to write them himself. To help him out—and to also help himself to meet his writing commitments—Fearn invited Japp to write a complete synopsis of western novels, with notes on the main characters and action. Fearn then did all of the actual writing, and privately paid Japp 25% of his income from the eventual sale of the books. The arrangement worked well, and no less than six collaborative westerns were quickly published by Scion Ltd. between February and October 1950: *Bonanza*, *Firewater*, *Ghost Canyon*, *Lead Law*, *Rattlesnake*, and *Skeleton Pass*.

Their collaborations then came to an end when Fearn signed a contract with Scion to write science fiction exclusively. But Fearn had encouraged Japp to attempt to write his own western novel, and he completed a book entitled *Jackson's Spread*, which he sold to Brown Watson Ltd. in 1952.

After the sale, Japp waited eagerly for his first book to come out, but he never heard another thing from the publisher. As time passed, he was forced to the realisation that the book must never have been published. Discouraged, he gave up writing and concentrated on building up his grocery business,

In 1968, Philip Harbottle's biblio-biography of John Russell Fearn, *The Multi-Man*, was publicised in a Blackpool newspaper, and Harbottle was contacted by many of Fearn's former friends, including Matt Japp. Harbottle travelled to Blackpool to meet him and his wife Nini, and they became friends. Japp was able to supply many anecdotes, letters, and documents revealing valuable information about Fearn's writings that enabled Harbottle to eventually uncover and track down hitherto unknown pseudonymous works by Fearn. Grateful for Japp's assistance in finding hitherto unknown stories by Fearn, Harbottle offered to research whether or not *Jackson's Spread* had ever been published by Brown Watson Ltd. He had a suspicion that it *had* been, but under a changed title and house name. He made a copy of its opening chapter from Japp's own carbon copy, and set to work on a search that would take more than a dozen years before he discovered that it had been published in 1952 as *Sudden Death* under the house name of Paul Daner. In common with many of the small "mushroom" publishers, Brown Watson never sent out complimentary copies or notified their authors of title and byline changes (standard practice at the time)

Japp was delighted when Harbottle presented him with the copy. He was even more delighted in 2000 when Harbottle—having only recently found a second copy of the extremely rare book—submitted it to the UK hardcover publisher Robert Hale Ltd, and sold it. Hale published it under the new title of *The Rancher's Revenge*, this time under Japp's own name. Robert Hale would also republish some two dozen Fearn westerns, including his six collaborations with Japp.

Ghost Canyon is the first of this amazing centenarian's westerns to be published in the USA, and others are in preparation.

www.ingramcontent.com/pod-product-compliance
Lightning Source LLC
Chambersburg PA
CBHW050738250626
47155CB00005B/1830